Books by Jennifer Kacey

Hot Wife

Our Rules

I0542059

Our Rules

ISBN # 978-1-78686-143-6

©Copyright Jennifer Kacey 2017

Cover Art by Posh Gosh ©Copyright 2017

Interior text design by Claire Siemaszkiewicz

Totally Bound Publishing

Published in 2017 by Totally Bound Publishing, Think Tank, Ruston Way, Lincoln, LN6 7FL, United Kingdom.

Hot Wife

OUR RULES

JENNIFER KACEY

Dedication

To You. And Our rules. Every word of this book is Yours.
Love you morerererer!

Chapter One

Wesley

Tabitha's urgent voicemail bled into Wes' veins as he listened to it for the second time. Pumping hard, his heartrate jacked his need for her even higher. The hushed timbre of her voice never failed to call to him, plead with him.

"I need to see you tonight. I've been thinking about our date this weekend for days and I know I won't be able to stop obsessing until I see you."

Closing his eyes for a second, he pictured her cherry-red nipples hardening beneath her staid blouse. She was a CPA for a financial company and was always dressed so proper. He knew her pussy would be wet beneath her knee-length skirt. Her pupils would already be dilated, as if he'd been working her over for hours. Torturing her body with such exquisite pleasure it bordered on pain was something he needed. Something he craved. Something very few women had been able to handle more than once.

But his bottom Tabitha?

That sexy dynamo with her hair in a bun wore prim pinstriped skirts and could always take him. She craved him. Needed his dominance as if it was air. His cock jerked behind his slacks, more than ready to be let out to play.

Her breathing sped up on the message. "Please, Wes. I know we aren't supposed to meet until Saturday night but I can't wait. I'm so wet I've already had to go to the ladies' room and clean up twice this morning. It's only a few minutes past ten." Her voice gained an octave at the end, clearly affected by her reaction to him.

As if he needed another reason to want to see her.

"I ache for you. Michael isn't due back until nine tonight. Please," she whispered, and abruptly the connection dropped.

Michael.

Her husband.

Hunger ate at his insides. The need to control the beautiful woman who'd left the message grew with every second that ticked by.

As he opened his eyes, Wes stared out of the twenty-fifth story window of his office building in downtown Jacksonville, North Carolina. As he stood in the conference room before anyone else arrived, he barely resisted the urge to replay the message again. Instead he exited his voicemail and checked his watch.

It had already been one hell of a busy day. Half past one o'clock stared back at him from the face of his Breitling Chronomat 41. Didn't take him thirty seconds to mentally run through the rest of his day and figure out what he could shuffle around to make room for…more pressing endeavors.

First, a meeting with his project managers on the new government contract they'd been awarded the Monday before was scheduled to start in just a few minutes. Then another consultation with his engineers in a couple of hours on a new drone prototype they were about to start work on. Then one last update with his board of directors, from which they were going to depart very happy.

He had plans with a buddy of his to catch a championship fight in Charlotte later that night. It wasn't supposed to start until nine, but they still had to take the jet to get there. *Hmm…*

His dick pulsed again, reminding him that he'd already made the decision so he might as well move along with altering plans. Tabitha on her knees or bound beneath him, his handprint on her ass. Simplest decision he'd made all day.

She should already be back to work and unable to answer her cell at her desk if she'd left for lunch.

Perfect.

Pulling up her contact information, under Tabby Cat, took him about two seconds. He'd nicknamed her that for two reasons after the first time he'd fucked her.

One, because she had the prettiest pussy he'd ever seen. Small lips, super sensitive and one of the most gorgeous shades of fuckable he'd been able to lay his tongue on. And two, since she purred when a certain man had her.

His cock jerked.

Almost three years ago, he'd sunk inside her slick heat, and he still hadn't gotten enough.

Being allergic to monogamy normally had him moving on, and quick. Even from women such as Tabitha who were otherwise spoken for.

But something about her called to him. Her ability to submit to him so effortlessly, maybe. Possibly her capacity to blossom beneath his command. Beneath his pain. His need to control her grew each time he laid eyes on her, and the ways she danced in his rope could fill a library of books.

Submission wasn't something a person could learn. Nor was dominance.

Not in his way of thinking.

There was something about how his Tabby Cat knelt naked at his feet he couldn't ignore. *Wouldn't* ignore. But this was the first time she'd called up out of the blue to meet with him. 'Dates' were normally planned at least two weeks in advance. Sometimes he met her at her house and sometimes at a hotel of her choosing.

Both places were equally intense and turned him on so damn fast. Normally, by the time he closed the door he had to fuck her, before they ever made it to a bed.

She liked it dirty.

Rough.

And she was his to command.

That she'd called him up in the middle of the day to meet that night probably should have made him pause, but it didn't. Life was too short for too much thinking about certain details. Sex with their kind of power exchange definitely fell into that category for him. Tabitha was so hot and he was so horny for her that he was game as soon as he'd seen it was her who had left a message. Her desire raced beneath his flesh and his cock twitched again.

Hearing people exit the elevator at the far end of the floor, he swiped the screen of his phone to place the call and grinned when her voicemail picked up immediately. *Good.* And he hoped she saw it was him calling. Anticipation turned her on something hardcore. Lucky girl. Because he was ready to play and 'aggressive' was going to be the main attraction.

Her bouncy voice reached him through the phone. "Hi! This is Tabitha. Leave me a message and I'll call you back. Byyeeeeee."

Beep.

"Pink fuck-me heels, black garter, black thigh-highs and no panties. Nothing else. I want your hair up in the bun you wore for work today. I'll take it down when I decide to. At half past eight I want you on all fours on your husband's bed with your pussy and ass facing the door. I'll let myself in downstairs with the spare key. Your fingers on your pussy to get your slit nice and wet for me. Understand? Text me back the only two words I want to hear. Gonna use each hole. Hope you're ready."

Just as he hung up, voices in the hallway reached him. Stepping up to the head of the table to hide his hard-on, he took a seat. Eleven of his top project managers filed into the boardroom. He set his phone in front of him and switched it to silent.

"Of course, he's already here," Sinclair, one of his newest hires, confirmed with a grin as soon as he sat. "Wes, do you ever sleep?"

There were rumors going around the office that all Wes

did was work. *If they only knew the half of my extracurricular activities.* "I'll sleep when I'm dead."

Everyone chuckled as they got settled and most of them picked up the thick packets of information already sitting at each of their locations.

"Let's go ahead and get started. Contrary to popular belief, I actually have plans tonight that do not involve business. I can't miss them, so let's get right to it." He hoped they could be professional and focus, but…no such luck.

"Oh, my God. I hope someone was secretly videoing that," Sinclair mock-whispered.

"We could win the pool if we prove he's actually human," a smiling woman on Sinclair's left mumbled behind her hand. Ericka had been with him for almost five years. She was loyal, wicked smart and *can't* wasn't in her vocabulary when he brought a project to her he wanted handled.

He grinned. "Guess you'll all have to be faster on the draw next time."

"Dammit," an older gentlemen on his right cursed as he set his phone back down. "I'll get you my pretty, and your little dog, too."

Everybody laughed, including Wes. "Hector, you just nominated yourself to turn the lights off."

The man stood with mock outrage. "You're only trying to keep my people down."

"What people?" somebody else joked. "Your family's been here longer than any of ours."

Another woman, sitting next to him, shooed him toward the door. "I've been to your houses. Both of them. You have a housekeeper. So, shut it!"

Everyone else heckled him as he headed toward the set of light switches by the door.

"Ericka," Wes spoke her name softly as the jabs continued.

His other project manager, set to lead the meeting, swiveled around and faced him. "Yeah, boss?"

"They're all yours." He slid the remote control across the table. "Bring them up to speed on Phase I and I'll fill in anywhere you need me to."

She petted the remote. "My precious."

"Oh, Lordy. Ericka has the remote."

"Save yourself," Sinclair added.

Wes shook his head and smirked one more time. "It's a wonder you guys get anything done."

Hector pointed to his chest. "That hurts right here."

Ericka laughed and brought up the first slide on the projector that shone on the wall ahead of Wes. Everyone chuckled, faced that direction, and finally got down to business. They might play hard but they worked hard, too. Wes, of all people, could respect that.

Twenty minutes later, Wes' phone display lit up, signaling he'd received a text message. Licking his bottom lip, he could almost taste Tabitha's sweet juices on his mouth. He ran his thumb across the screen and pulled up his messages.

Yes, Sir.

The exact two words he'd been waiting for pumped through his veins, reminding him of what would be waiting after work.

A very capable, intelligent and racy as hell woman waiting to take what dirty and delicious things he wanted to do to her.

Power surged through him, pressing him to take action.

Good girl, he texted back before turning off his screen and pocketing the phone.

He flipped another page on the packet as everyone else around the table did, determined to fully participate in the meeting continuing all around him.

The timing of him tuning back in couldn't have been better.

Ericka turned to him, as did everyone else. "Wes, do you know the projected start date on Phase I construction so we have an idea how long we have for the infrastructure prep?"

"Three months. It's gonna be tight."

"Who are we using for this one?" Sinclair asked.

"Graves Design and Construction. We've worked with him before. I don't anticipate any delays so we need to get on this immediately."

Affirmatives followed his statement and they all looked back up at the next slide.

Graves Design and Construction.

As in Michael Graves.

Wes smiled.

Tabitha's husband.

Chapter Two

Wesley

The scene waiting for him as he silently pushed open Tabitha's bedroom door at precisely eight-thirty kicked his dominant cravings to the forefront.

On her hands and knees, just as he'd told her. Her bare pussy on display, facing the door like he'd directed, made his balls ache. She rubbed her clit in tight little circles, eliciting a full-fledged growl as he stepped inside.

Tabitha *eeked* and glanced over her shoulder at him.

Tossing his suit coat toward a chair off to one side, he had no idea if it landed on top. He didn't look long enough to tell.

The light from her bedside lamp highlighted half of her face and body, creating dips and shadows he couldn't wait to explore.

He pushed the door closed and watched her.

Color filled her cheeks as he stared at her pussy. "Both hands on the bed, Tabby Cat. I'll be using that pussy now."

The black material of her stockings and garters highlighted her tanned skin when she shifted to place her other palm on the pristine white comforter beneath her. A rich shade of purple on the walls, her favorite hue, surrounded them within an ambiance of decadence and desire. Her shoulders lifted as she inhaled, and she tracked his movements across the room. He emptied his pockets on her tall dresser.

Her eyes. Beautiful.

Brown and gold swirled together to form a perfect combination of temptation and innocence.

The pose?

Completely submissive, trusting, open.

But her eyes?

Provocative, seductive, fierce.

The dual sides of her personality spoke to him. Called to him. Begged for him.

It was a scream inside his head to take. Possess. Control. All of her.

From the top of her bun all the way down to her curled toes.

He wanted it all and he was going to have it.

"Do you know how hard you make me when you follow my instructions? How badly I want to fuck you senseless with that prim little bun in your hair?" Closing the distance between them, he stared at the gorgeous brown-haired woman laid out before him as if she were a meal.

Thin, with curves in all the right places, she was definitely his kind of poison.

He planned to have his fill and more before the night was done.

"Maybe," she answered and smiled.

"Safe word is the same as always?"

She nodded. "Rutabaga."

"And if I have something shoved in that tempting little mouth of yours, you do what if you need to stop?"

She raised one hand, the same one she'd had on her pussy, and snapped her fingers.

"Good. Now, I want my handprint on you." Without pausing, he crashed his hand down onto the flesh of her ass then again on the other cheek.

Tabitha jerked her hips to the side on each swat as she planted her hands. A natural reaction with no additional warning from him, but it made him growl again.

Moving, even if it was nothing more than an automatic response, had him baring his teeth. "Don't move away from me. Don't deny me." Her withholding what he wanted pissed him off. Fair or not didn't matter. "Give me what I want, Tabby Cat," he roared with greed as he stepped up to the end of the bed her head was on.

"Yes, Sir." Her gaze met his. She shivered and bit her bottom lip as she stared at him.

Fuck, she turned him on.

As she eyed him, she licked her lips, glancing up at him and back down to the tent his cock made just for her.

Throughout his life in and around the kink scene, he'd met many dominant individuals who required the people playing with them to keep their eyes downcast, subservient.

But that had never been one of his kinks.

He wanted to see each emotion play across his partner's features. Even the ones they tried to hide. Those were the most delicious.

A pushover turned him off faster than anything. He didn't want a lapdog, he wanted a challenge.

Pulling a reaction from Tabitha when fought not to give in made his cock throb. Hard.

Making her respond. Now, that was most definitely one of his kinks.

The fact she was married pushed his need for her even higher. Being a saint had never interested him. But being a kinky bastard? *Hell, yeah.*

"Keep your palms on the bed. Mouth only. No hands. I want to feel every inch of you as I get closer and closer to fucking your throat." After yanking off his tie, he tossed it on the bed by her feet and made quick work of his zipper before he pulled out his throbbing shaft. "Open up. Oh. Fuck. Your mouth. Fuck."

A tremor worked up his spine as she slid her lips along his shaft.

She was so dirty, almost naked, bare breasted with her lips wrapped around him.

Her moan made him want to howl.

"You were all wet, Sir." She whispered the words against his cock as he pointed it at her. She licked the head and moaned, a slight shiver working along her torso.

"Have been all day, ever since you left that voicemail. My dick stayed wet for hours. I needed my Tabby Cat to clean it up."

Bobbing up and down on his shaft, she hummed against his tight flesh. "Needed you all day. So horny." She licked the tip then swirled her tongue around the head of his cock and smiled.

"Happy with my cock in your mouth?" He only asked because he wanted to hear her answer. See it. Feel it.

"So happy, Sir." Her eyes closed and another tremor vibrated down her body.

"And are you wet for me?" He didn't wait for her to answer. He paused as he reached over her, then slid his fingers through the wetness coating the lips of her pussy. "Fuck. You're drenched."

"All day. Dripping."

"It's even soaked your thighs now. So wet."

"Desperate," she whispered as she moved on his cock. "Wanted to come so bad at work, but…"

Wes traced the lips of her sex with the tips of his fingers, knowing he wasn't giving her near the friction she needed to get off. When he filled her he wanted her needy, frantic. The way her hips jerked each time he grazed her clit, he didn't think it would take her long to get there. But he still wanted to make her come. Emphasis on *make*.

"You know I'm going to spank your ass red for calling me today, don't you?"

Her mouth momentarily went slack and a whine, barely audible, reached his ears. "But…I thought I was supposed to tell you if I could meet earlier than our date? Thought I was doing what you asked?" Her eyebrows pulled low in what he thought was concentration and he ran the head of his dick along her bottom lip. She kissed the tip and resumed the steady up and down on his shaft.

"You did."

She tried to pull off again but he grabbed her bun and forced his cock to the back of her throat. Holding her there almost sucked the cum from his balls. Another rumble worked its way free of his chest. "Don't stop again unless I tell you to." He controlled her movement as he gritted his teeth and convinced his own body not to come.

That was what she did to him.

She called the beast inside him free. Sometimes he had to chain him again if he couldn't control the need rioting through his limbs.

Plus, he wasn't done teasing her yet.

With a tight fist in her hair, he pushed in a little deeper. Then a bit more until she gagged, and he yanked her off.

She sucked air in and out of her lungs as she tried to catch her breath. He didn't give her long before he pushed the fat head past her lips again.

"Lick under the head. Just like that. Your wicked tongue is gonna get you used." He pumped his hips, fucking her mouth with his cock. His balls tingled as liquid spilled from her core onto his fingers. He continued to torment the swollen lips of her sex and she moaned around his shaft. "I'm going to spank your ass till you beg me to stop. I'm going to spank it because you did exactly what you were supposed to do. What you had permission to do. I'm going to let you wear my handprint because you've been a very good girl. And good girls get rewards." He pushed into her throat and paused as he strummed her clit.

Her feet shifted against the comforter and her back bowed.

She fought to get away and he fucking loved it. Consent was one of the sexiest things about kink.

Fight or flight kicked in at some point when she couldn't breathe, and he pushed in a little farther.

To her credit, her hands never came off the bed. Her fingers stretched and twisted but she never once disobeyed his order.

He yanked her off his cock and she sucked great pulls of oxygen into her lungs. Releasing her now messy bun, he didn't give her any chance to relax before pushing her.

She didn't resist him as he shoved her upper body on to the

bed. She didn't fight him. She did nothing but beautifully submitted to what he needed. Pre-cum shot from the tip of his cock. It landed on her ribcage as she groaned, rolling her forehead back and forth against the comforter.

As he let her try to regain her bearings, he moved to the end of the bed and tugged her hips backward until her sultry pink heels hung off the edge.

"I've never seen you so wet, Tabby Cat. Such a pretty pussy." He slid a finger into her sex, deep, deeper, until she moaned into the comforter.

She grabbed handfuls of the white fabric and he remembered his tie.

"Arms behind your back."

He snatched up the tie as she slowly complied. Two knots later her wrists were bound at the small of her back, which pushed her ass inch by inch closer to him.

Just where he wanted it.

Untucking and unbuttoning his shirt took only a few seconds. He growled when the last button wouldn't let go and he ripped the two halves apart. The round disk pinged off the hard wood floor before hitting the wall somewhere.

Filling her with two thick fingers made more blood rush to his cock. The slick sides of her pussy fluttered around his invading digits.

"Already need to come?"

"Yes," she whispered.

"Yes?" he repeated. "Yes, what?" Wrenching his fingers free, there was no pause before he slapped her ass half a dozen times. The wetness from her pussy juice heightened the contact and his hand tingled by the time he pushed his fingers back inside her channel.

"Yes, Sir. Yes. Sir." She huffed out on each word. "Need to come so bad. Please," she pleaded in the same desperate whisper she'd used on the phone.

"I love it when you beg to come."

"Please, Sir. Please, please. I need it." Her fingers constantly moved, clenching and unclenching as he stretched her opening to take him.

He yanked the end of his belt free and released the button and fly on his slacks. He thought about stopping to get undressed but the thought only lasted a moment. The idea of fucking her as he stood almost fully clothed seriously did it for him.

Fingerfucking her with one hand, he fisted his cock with the other and stroked himself a couple times. He needed inside her. Needed to invade her holes the way she'd invaded his thoughts ever since she'd left that message for him.

Riding her G-spot with the tips of two fingers turned him on. The tiny ridges of her sex were filled with fluid and the walls of her pussy shimmied again. Making her squirt hadn't been on his radar but now it sure was.

"Fuck," she cursed as he rolled his thumb across her clit. The hard little nub quivered beneath the pad of his thumb. Sliding his fingers through her slickness made her vibrate with need.

"Did you come at work today? Did you take that little vibrator out of your makeup bag I know you keep with you and go to the ladies' room? Did you make this pussy come, thinking about tonight? About me fucking you on the bed you share with your husband?"

"No," rushed out of her. "I wanted to. Wanted to get away to take care of myself but I was so busy. Thought about it again on the way home. Driving!" she yelled. "I don't do things like that." The muscles in her back pulled tight as he pushed a third finger into her small hole.

"What's the real reason you didn't jill and get yourself off?"

"I don't know," tore past her lips as she circled her hips in time with his thumb on her clit.

"Sure you do. It's very simple." He moved his hand up and pushed at the mound of her sex, exposing her clit even more. "Why didn't you come today at work? Or on the way home? Or in here before I arrived? You could have found two minutes to get off. Probably wouldn't have taken you more than thirty seconds in the ladies' room with your tiny panties pulled to the side. Why didn't you come? I'll let you come as soon as you own why you didn't find the time to get off."

She shook her head back and forth again, squeezing her hands into little fists.

He pushed his fingers in deep and…paused. Holding his breath, he waited for the words he knew she would speak.

"I didn't want to come by my own hand. I wanted you to make me come, Sir. I wanted to give it to you." Her soft words called forth the darkness inside him.

"Because it's mine, isn't that right, Tabby Cat? When you need a bite of pain it's more than just the act, isn't it? I'm in that pretty little head of yours as well as in your tight snatch." He didn't ask the last part. It wasn't a question. He knew exactly what she needed even if she didn't.

"Yes, Sir."

But hearing her admit it? *Damn.*

Her coming with just his fingers didn't do it for him anymore. Watching her come instead of feeling her shudder on his cock wasn't good enough.

He needed more.

No. He needed everything she had to give him.

After wrenching his hands free, he jerked her knees out from beneath her and her bottom half collapsed onto the mattress.

"Sir?" she asked as she tried to get her knees beneath her and look over her shoulder.

He shoved her legs apart, and held her down by a hand between her shoulders. The beautiful slick lips between her thighs taunted him.

He shoved his pants down a few inches and fitted the head of his cock to her pussy. Thrusting inside shorted out his brain.

Her pussy locked down on him halfway in and he blanketed her body, putting most of his weight on her. "So fucking soft," he whispered against her neck as the flesh of his chest rubbed against her back and her bound arms. With a fist in her hair, he bit her shoulder until she shrieked. He retreated and pushed into her again and again. "Let me in, damn you. Let. Me. In."

He fucked her harder onto the bed, pushing his free hand beneath her to get to her clit. "Come on my cock. I want it. Give it to me."

Tabitha opened her mouth and her eyelids fluttered closed as her pussy clamped down on him again. Clench, release, clench, release. He thrummed the tight bundle of nerves and licked the bite mark on her shoulder. She screamed as she came. Her body twisted so hard she almost knocked him off as he continued to pump inside her.

"Sir," she cried as he fucked her. Her hips twitched beneath him as if she had no control over them, meeting him thrust for thrust.

Sensation built at the base of his spine and he knew he wasn't going to be able to hold off much longer. He reached between them then quickly freed her wrists and tossed his tie on the floor beside the bed.

He moved her hands from behind and wrapped his arms around her. Using her body, he fucked her even harder.

"So. Hard," she said through gritted teeth, and held onto his forearms.

"Like stone." He drove his length inside her once, twice. "I'm gonna come inside you. I'm gonna fill up that greedy little pussy of yours. And I know I said I was going to use all three holes but I think I'll leave your ass alone so your husband can fuck it tonight. Using my cum as lube." He whispered the last sentence in her ear and her entire body shook as she groaned. "Like that, don't you." It wasn't really a question. "So dirty." He licked her throat.

"Fuck. Sir. Please," she begged.

Sensation bubbled in his veins as her core tightened around him again. "Are you ready for my cum, you dirty girl?"

"Yes, Sir," she moaned.

He rode her G-spot, pushing her into another orgasm, and her mouth fell open in a silent scream.

His balls sucked up to his body and his vision went black. Reality paused all around him.

In the next second, his world exploded as pure pleasure raced down his spine. Cum jetted from the tip of his cock and Tabitha yelled again and clawed at him.

To get closer or get away, he didn't know.

Holding on, he kept her right where he wanted her.

His cock throbbed and her pussy seemed to kiss every inch of him inside her.

But his heart stopped in his chest as the door flew open behind them, bouncing off the wall.

"What the hell is going on here?" a deep voice bellowed. A voice belonging to only one person.

Tabitha's husband.

Michael's face was an unreadable mask as he stared at them on the bed.

Another pulse of cum shot out of Wes' dick. He continued to throb inside her. He gritted his teeth as he loosened his hold on her and pushed himself up on his elbows. Three more thrusts. He punctuated each word with, "Fucking. Your. Wife."

And at that, Tabitha giggled and wrinkled her nose. She smiled at her husband, extending her hand to him when he moved forward.

He grinned and shook his head. Brushing hair from her face, he leaned down and kissed her cheek. "Hottest. Wife. Ever."

Which was a title Tabitha wore with hedonistic pride.

Michael's — hot — wife.

Chapter Three

Tabitha

Tabitha sighed as Wes pulled out, and she curled her toes as some of his cum spilled free from her pussy. The thick liquid coated the lips of her sex and dripped off her clit as Wes moved off the bed.

Nothing made her feel dirtier or more delicious than another man's cum leaking from her pussy.

No.

That was wrong.

Only one thing made her feel dirtier. When her husband climbed on the bed next to her and spread her legs to watch it happen.

"My. What filthy holes you have, wife?"

"No, my husband. What filthy holes *you* have." She tucked her arms beneath her almost naked body as Michael slid his fingers through the wetness.

She never called her husband 'Sir'. Not ever. Once when they'd first gotten together she'd used the honorific to address him when he was spanking her, but the use of 'Sir' had hit them both wrong.

"Too impersonal," he'd said. His name on her lips was what he wanted to hear. Needed to hear. Then, later, when he let her play with others, he'd said how much he liked hearing her call them 'Sir'. That step away from them emotionally was ideal.

Made her even more his.

She and Michael still played rough. Not as hard as she did with Wes or Duke, one of the other guys she got to play with, but rough. Michael's need to hurt her had changed over the years. Lessened. He said it had changed when his need to protect her intensified.

But he understood her desire for the pain sometimes and he made sure she got what she needed.

His providing for her sexually made submitting to him that much more fulfilling—and terrifying because it involved her emotions.

The power exchange between her and Wes was delicious and sexy because of the dirty fun they got to have, but that was where it ended. If he walked away, she'd be sad but intact.

The D/s relationship she had with Michael was just… more. Her emotional safety was intertwined with their dynamic. Dependent on it, even. Thinking about it sometimes scared her, but he was always there to catch her if she needed him to.

Their connection made him even that much more amazing.

"Hell yes, I do. Very, very dirty holes." He spread the creamy fluid up to her asshole and ringed the tight hole.

She moaned as he dipped a finger inside her ass, and arched her back to keep him inside as long as possible when he pulled free.

"As always, I thank you for a most entertaining evening." Wes clapped Michael on the shoulder.

"You're very welcome. Love how you use her. She's always so pliable when you get done. She likes your edge."

"And I like hers. Fuck, do I." Wes stepped in front of her and she lifted her head for a kiss. He'd already pulled on his slacks and attached his belt once again, but the material of his shirt hung loosely off his shoulders. His tie draped around his collar was totally hot. The gap of his shirt highlighted his six pack and happy trail. And it represented *her* trail of happy.

"Amazing as always, Tabby Cat." He kissed her mouth and dipped his tongue inside.

Just a taste, but it made her pussy contract nonetheless.

She bit her bottom lip. "Best Tuesday night I've had in a while. Not your usual schedule, but I'd sure be up for more of it if you both are."

"Sorry for the short notice, but I wanted to surprise Michael with something extra naughty when he got home. He's been working really late nights for the last while. Thought he could use a little bit of distraction."

"Mission accomplished." Michael touched the small of her back and moved between her thighs.

"So, you used me?" Wes seemed to feign offense.

"Yep," Tabitha answered with a smile.

"Cheeky girl," Wes teased with a laugh and wiggled the bun that was sort of still together at the back of her head.

She blew hair out of her eyes and he helped tuck it behind her ear.

She stared at her husband over her shoulder as he loosened his tie and tossed it onto the mattress. As Michael untucked his shirt, Wes brushed more hair off her cheek then removed all the hairpins from her bun.

A sigh slipped from between her lips as Wes massaged her scalp and Michael fit the head of his cock against the fluttering entrance to her pussy. She moaned as he pushed her legs farther apart.

"Which one of us was that for, Tabby?" Michael asked, slowly thrusting inside. "Such a tight pussy even after it's already been taken tonight."

She grabbed a handful of the covers beneath her as Michael's dirty words slithered inside her head. She stretched to get closer to both men. A purr slipped out as Michael pulled back and thrust in one more time.

"Hence the nickname," Wes chuckled.

She'd purred for Michael as long as they'd been together. Even the first night he'd kissed her she'd purred. No clue why she did it for him and no one else, but he loved it. And so did she.

Even when he let her fuck other guys, the purr was all for him.

Tabitha loved it when Michael called her Tabby.

Wes had nicknamed her Tabby Cat after the first time he'd heard her purr for her husband. That had been the first time they'd fooled around together.

So delicious.

She bit her lip as Michael circled her asshole with his thumb again.

"Oh, fuck," Wes cursed. "I'd better get out of here or I'm going to be up for round two. Pun intended."

"I'm sure Tabby wouldn't mind." Her husband glanced over and raised his eyebrows.

She looked up at Wes and his face was free of any emotion, as it normally was. Such a hard face to read, except when he was coming inside her. Then she understood him so clearly. "Want to stay, Sir?" She licked her lips and glanced at the fly of his slacks, which had already tented a bit.

He flipped his wrist over and stared at his watch for a second. "Let me make a call and I'll be right back." He tightened his fist in her hair for a second.

"Fuck. She just squeezed my dick and got so wet. So dirty, my hot wife."

Wes stepped out of the bedroom and Tabitha laid her head back down on the bed.

A hot wife.

Not something she'd known to put a name to when she and Michael had gotten together five years prior, but they'd soon found they had similar proclivities.

She liked multiple partners, the dirty aspect of it, the sharing, and that she was a possession to her husband. That he could loan her out as he saw fit, which made their sex life off-the-charts wickedly erotic.

He liked claiming her, possessing her, fucking her with another man's cum as lube.

And sometimes she got to have her husband and her date. Not all the time, but sometimes she was super fortunate. Sometimes it seemed her luck was unending. *Tonight may just be one of those nights, when I get to have another round and*

my husband gets the dirty fun of watching another man fuck my
mouth as he stretches out my ass.

And Wes?

He wasn't the only guy she got to have sex with.

One of her favorites — absolutely.

But not the only one.

Glancing over her shoulder, she stared at the man she belonged to. Her heart tripped over itself to beat faster.

Her husband.

Her everything.

"Good thing you don't have panties on, my wife. Such a good girl." Staring down at her, his gaze spoke of love and cleared her mind of all but him. In the handful of years they'd spent together, he'd joked about rules she had to follow, some nothing but dirty fun. One of his favorite *rules* was no panties so he could take her any time he wanted to.

Others had changed over time. Condoms for all dates — for everyone but him. But they'd decided him using other men's cum to fuck her turned them both on.

Several other rules were very serious. He'd never break a promise. He'd always be there to reconnect after a date. And he'd never use her emotions against her.

That last one wrecked her.

Her head knew he would never do that, but her heart still had a hard time believing it sometimes.

Those pseudo-rules had become a kind of mantra. Something to hold close around herself if she felt lost or afraid.

Heat filtered through her body as Michael took her. "Fuck, I love you," he whispered as he thrust inside. "You beneath me. Me taking you back. Mine."

Him saying the words she craved filled her with so much love and thankfulness she thought she might burst with them. Reconnecting after someone else had been inside her had become something she depended on more than she thought possible. It was a very important constant that had developed over the years of their marriage and further cemented their dynamic.

In her purse, she carried a piece of paper with the '*rules*' written down. No more than a handful of items she kept close, but they kept her grounded. Kept her safe. She'd looked at the simple reminders so many times she had them memorized, but the information was something she'd put together. Not *they'd* put together. The rules weren't really rules. More of an inside joke.

Dozens of times she'd thought to show Michael but she just hadn't. Honestly, she felt lame needing some kind of talisman with her to remind her of how far she'd come. How far they'd come. Her ex-boyfriend had left scars *so* deep when he'd broken her heart, and she still had to fight not to run when things got hard.

But she was doing better.

Michael helped her *be* better.

"Up on your knees, gorgeous. I want ass. Fuck, you make me so hard."

He lifted her up, but planted a hand between her shoulder blades to keep her upper body on the bed.

"I love it when you put me where you want me."

"Love that you follow my commands, no matter if they're verbal or physical. I love playing with you. Love fucking you. Making love to you. Everything. Every minute. I've missed you lately." He leaned over her back and wrapped one of his arms around her, holding her to him.

"Missed you, too." Much more than she wanted to admit.

"Gonna get lube. Don't go anywhere." He licked her cheek and she smiled.

She watched him as he moved to the nightstand to find the lube.

A couple of years prior, he'd been working at a very high-profile architectural firm. Highbrow, good pay, standard hours. A few years before that, when he'd been at the same job, was actually how they'd met. But he hadn't been happy there so they'd talked about him branching off and starting his own firm.

They'd saved and talked about it some more — and talked some more.

They were in the outskirts of Jacksonville, North Carolina, which was a very diverse location with a huge amount of growth potential.

She had a good job as a CPA, so they'd decided he should go for it.

And he had.

Talk. About. Busy.

Almost all of his clients had gone with him, and most were multi-locational government or philanthropic organizations.

He stayed busy, all the time. He'd hired a receptionist-slash-secretary. He had several draftsmen, too, but a lot of the design work still fell to him. Then there were the projects actually under construction. He had several foremen who oversaw the jobs, but he was very hands-on with all of it.

It meant late nights and early mornings, and she missed him. A lot.

He grabbed the lube, curled his fingers around it and squeezed some on his cock then climbed back behind her on the bed.

She shivered beneath him as he filled her pussy once again, then leaned over to rub his stubble up her spine. "I love your five o'clock shadow. Have I ever told you that?"

They both laughed. It was a bit of a joke.

She told him every time he brushed his stubble against her.

Talk about a yummy trigger.

"Once or twice," he whispered against the flesh of her back. He glanced at the door and she followed his gaze. "Looks like someone's been a very good girl lately. Or very naughty," he added as Wes stepped back into the bedroom.

Michael straightened and rubbed the excess lube from his hands on her ass. Her date approached her side of the bed, where her head was pressed against the mattress.

"I have twenty minutes before I have to be out of here."

Wes moved his shirt tails out of the way and unzipped his pants. He pulled his half-hard cock out just as Michael slid his thumb deep inside her ass.

"Oh, fuck," she mumbled as Wes pressed the head of his cock between her lips.

"Twenty minutes, Tabby Cat. So, you're gonna have to work for it, since I just blew my load in that tight pussy of yours."

She licked him from root to tip, sucking at the end. "No worries, Sir." Closing her eyes, she surrendered herself to the decadent position most people only dreamed about. She knew how amazing her life was and didn't take it for granted.

Not for a second.

"I'll even sweeten the deal," Michael added. "You make him come and I'll make you come. Can't beat that."

"But I want your cum, my husband. Badly," she mumbled against Wes' cock. She wasn't above begging for what she needed.

"You'll get it. Seems to me, two of your three holes will be full. Believe it will be up to me to take care of the third one." He pulled his thumb free, then filled her ass with a finger. Two.

"Fuuccckkk," she cursed as she licked a drop of pre-cum from Wes' cock.

"It's a dirty job, but somebody's gotta do it. I'd be happy to round out your holy trinity of filth tonight, my wife. It would be my honor to take care of you."

A vow. Those words were an oath. A promise he'd made to her on their wedding day. They never failed to render her blissfully happy, and she purred along Wes' shaft as he slid in again. Deeper. Stronger.

Her consciousness floated free as Michael fucked her pussy and fingered her ass, and she relaxed into his keeping.

Ung, ung, ung, was the sound she made as Wes grabbed a handful of her hair and pushed into the back of her throat.

She sucked on the head of his dick each time he withdrew.

She knew what he liked. She knew what would get him off.

One thing sexy to her about new partners? Getting to discover what pushed their buttons.

And it was something altogether amazing to be with someone else multiple times, as she'd been with Wes. Learning more about what satisfied them. What harder edge they needed to get off more than once.

Tabitha closed her jaw the tiniest bit when Wes pulled out, knowing the scrape of her teeth along his shaft would push him closer to the edge.

"Fuck, those pointy teeth, Tabby Cat. Open your throat. I want in." The words were forced out through a tight jaw and she knew how close he already was.

She relaxed her throat as much as she could, because he'd fuck it anyway. There had been times in the past when she'd struggled because it was hot and dirty to fight a bit. He'd always overpowered her and she liked that.

"Your pussy just sucked me back in. Like it when he fucks your throat, sexy?" Michael gathered more wetness around his cock. Wes' cum and lube. That was what he spread around her ass and used to fuck her with.

Another man's cum.

She shivered as Wes grabbed the back of her head and forced his way into her throat. Yes, she gagged. No, she knew he definitely didn't mind.

"Jesus. I'm gonna come so hard. Put your hands on my balls, Tabby Cat."

Shifting to get her arm out from beneath her, she sucked in a huge breath. As soon as her fingers brushed his sac he pushed back into her throat. As she rolled his balls in her hand, he fucked her face. She struggled to breathe and thrashed around beneath her husband and lover.

They held her in place, using her. Together, they had an easy hundred and fifty pounds of muscle on her. Others may have felt scared or vulnerable.

Not Tabitha.

On her knees before them, she'd never felt more powerful.

Even as a tiny thread of fear weaved itself inside her mind.

She thought of her safe word and signal to use if she couldn't speak. Not to actually use either of them to stop the scene. She simply thought of them to know she didn't want to use them. Not with either of the men taking her.

Why would she stop something just because she was scared?

She trusted these men with her body, her mind. With all of her. If she didn't trust them completely she'd never let them touch her. Michael wouldn't let that happen, either. Ever.

So, she relished the moments where the rest of the world fell away and she could be who she was meant to be.

The submissive hot wife of an amazing man.

Michael pulled out of her and smacked her asshole with his cock.

The base nature of it turned her on. The way he pushed against her ass to get inside made her jerk. Hard.

"Oh, no, you don't," Wes admonished when she tried to shift away. He wrapped her free arm around to her back and held it there with his other fist still in her hair as he fucked her mouth.

Michael lifted the leg she didn't have the bulk of her weight on and pushed inside her ass. All the way. One. Long. Thrust.

She screamed around Wes' cock but it came out as a stuttering gurgle.

"Fuck, yes. Right there. Get ready to swallow my cum, Tabby Cat. Here it comes. Fuck, fuck." Wes paused in her mouth and she jerked so hard she dislodged Michael from her ass.

She inhaled as deeply as she could and swallowed as Wes filled her mouth. His cock spurted onto Tabitha's tongue and the back of her throat, and she swallowed the amazing elixir down. As she basked in the wanton liquid, something slid across her clit. Once and again.

"Uhhhhhh." She smiled as Wes pulled free, and she

shivered all the way down to her toes.

Michael had changed position. His head was between her spread thighs and he had his tongue on her clit.

So. Fucking. Dirty.

The slide of his mouth along those sensitive lips nearly pulled the orgasm from her. Then he latched on to the top of her pussy. Sucking and tonging her clit, he pushed her over the edge. She had no choice but to come. She bucked against his face and flipped over, unable to stay upright any longer. Michael rolled with her, never losing the suction on the tight bundle of nerves as an orgasm ripped her apart.

Zaps of sensation shot along Tabitha's nerves. The buzzing in her head was the most exquisite pleasure imaginable. Still jerking with orgasm, she was barely aware of Michael moving. He shoved her legs to her chest as he positioned his cock at the entrance to her sex. He pushed inside and they both groaned.

"Nothing is as good as fucking you, Tabby. Nothing."

Several strokes later he pulled out and tucked his slick cock to the tight circle of her ass. "Let me in, baby. I need inside you. Have to come. Can't wait any longer. Fuck, it's been too long since I've come in this ass. Take it. Give me what I need."

Since she was so wet, he slipped back into her pussy, and they moaned again.

Tabitha dug her nails into his knees because that was all she could touch. She needed her mark on him as surely as he marked her. Some things went both ways in their relationship. Their connection was amazing.

Pulling out again, he gave her a second to process what he needed, then tucked the head of his cock to her already sore back hole.

She took a deep breath and consciously relaxed.

Didn't take even a second for him to push inside.

Rough. Violent was what she was ready for. Prepared for.

Instead, he slowly claimed her ass.

And that was exactly what it was. A claiming.

He marked her as he took her. Possessed her as if he was branding her as his.

"Look at me," he growled as he pushed her legs to the sides.

She snapped her gaze to his as if magnetized by his words.

The cords in his neck stood out as he strained against her. He kept the pace slow and devastating. Fucking her ass as if he could keep it up for hours. Days, even. And he could. They loved it. Together, they could do anything.

"Beg me," he ground out as he buried his dick in her ass.

"Please, please, please. I need your cum. I can't live without it. Please. I need it." The words poured out of her as she grabbed the back of his neck and pulled him closer. "Please, my husband. Come in my ass. Fuck, I need it so bad. Please."

The first shot of cum startled them both.

Michael jerked once and collapsed on top of her, barely catching himself on his elbows before crushing her.

Tabitha cried out as she came and wrapped her legs around his body. She needed him like that. Raw. So deep she didn't know where he ended and she began.

His cum filled her ass for the next few thrusts and his head hit her shoulder. "Holy shit, Tabby. There is nothing that feels better than coming inside you. Nothing." He gathered her close and held her, pulsing inside her ass. He always made sure the rest of his load made it inside her.

That moment between them? That reconnection? It was... everything.

Tears threatened, but she didn't want to get emotional so she fought to keep it under control.

Tabitha blinked, and glanced up and around the room.

Wes was gone.

She smiled.

Great fuck. Great friend. He was there for the sex but didn't stick around for the emotional stuff, which suited all of them just fine.

She kissed Michael's shoulder and licked his throat.

Michael shifted, slipping free, and they both moaned. He flopped over onto his side and pulled her next to him with her head on his chest. "Gimme a few minutes, baby." He yawned so hard his jaw cracked. "So tired. Gimme a few minutes and I'll get you cleaned up."

She shifted against him and he jerked.

He looked as if he tried peel his eyelids open but she was pretty sure he was already mostly asleep.

"Let me get a washcloth and I'll clean you up this time, then I'm gonna shower. I'd ask you to join me but I'm pretty sure you'd fall over and I'm not strong enough to haul your butt back in here if you bite it."

"I could make it." His words slurred together, and she was pretty sure he was fully asleep before she even made it into the bathroom.

She came back in with a warm cloth and gently washed his mouth and his hands, then his cock and balls. It was a true testament to how tired he was that he never even moved.

Staring at him, she wondered how she'd survived without him. What had she done before him? Who had she told all her stuff to? Her dreams? Her fears?

He was her everything, even when things weren't… perfect.

She wandered back into the bathroom and turned on the hot water.

It only took a couple of minutes to do the rest of her nighttime routine and wrap her hair up into a less messy bun. Stepping under the hot water, she let the heat and steam loosen her stiff muscles.

Alone beneath the spray, her control slipped a bit and her emotions leaked out. She made fists against the wall and locked her jaw down to keep them in check as best she could.

Her ex-boyfriend had rewired part of her head when they'd been together, and she struggled sometimes in processing her feelings. She'd associated emotions with something negative for so long it was second nature, so she tended to shy away from them at all costs.

Then they tended to erupt, which scared her even worse.

She'd been raised by her no-fuss grandparents, who'd provided for her, but the love and affection hadn't been very apparent. She'd never known her father, and her mother had terminated her rights when Child Protective Services had pushed the issue after having to get involved more than a handful of times.

Tabitha didn't really remember her mother much. Just bits and pieces. But she'd survived and gotten a scholarship to college because of good grades. She was smart and liked math. Being a CPA came naturally to her. Being successful had taken her longer to wrap her head around, but she'd made her grandparents proud. After she was out on her own her grandparents hadn't lasted long. They'd died within months of each other. Natural causes for both, but it had hit her hard because they had been all the family she'd had left.

Right after they'd both passed, she'd met the ex. It hadn't been a healthy relationship, and she'd let it change her.

With Michael, she was better. He loved her and never made her feel less than when it came to being emotional with him. No matter how much time had passed, it was still a daily struggle. Even a handful of years later, she had to fight the urge to shut down. Her husband likened it to an addiction to alcohol or drugs. Shoving her emotions into a box made her feel safe. It helped her cope.

Unfortunately, it wasn't something she could walk away from like a bottle of bourbon. Her feelings weren't as easily gotten rid of or poured down the drain. She knew exactly how devastating addiction could be. She'd watched an uncle lose his battle with alcoholism when she was in high school.

They didn't make a twelve-step program for her with catchy sayings or a coin.

Michael was all of that for her. It had taken her years to

depend on him, trust him.

But lately he'd been so preoccupied she'd felt off-balance. More than once.

She hadn't admitted it. Not out loud. Sure as hell not to him.

Why would she have wanted to?

Pulling some kind of Chicken Little freak-out every time one of her triggers was brushed up against didn't do it for her. Not anymore. She did not like revealing her weaknesses. Ever.

Being strong on her own was sometimes too hard.

Standing beneath the spray of the water, no matter how hard she tried to get warm, cold fear crept in.

Things had always righted themselves before between herself and Michael. Always.

Until a few months or so before.

She'd wanted to know how much Michael was really paying attention. It was something that had always made her feel so special. And important. Treasured. Something she'd all of a sudden realized she'd been missing.

Bending the rules wasn't something she did to be mean or vindictive.

He had always been so on it when they were dating and for the first few years of their marriage.

It had been perfect until he'd branched off to start his own design and construction firm.

That was when everything changed.

And for the first time in their life together, he'd disappointed her. It wasn't big stuff. Not really. But she'd worn panties when he'd been home from work one night and he hadn't even noticed. Not even when she walked in front of him half naked, stripping the scrap of fabric off.

Not even the date with Wes tonight. She was supposed to give Michael at least twenty-four hours' notice of any sex date she had planned. Tonight? Twenty hours. She'd only given him twenty hours. She'd broken the rules and he hadn't even noticed.

It was all small things, tiny in the scheme of life, she thought as she let the water wash off her makeup.

But she'd grown to rely on the rules. To her they weren't funny. They were utterly important to her emotional balance, which made her feel stupid, but she couldn't depend on them any less.

There was even one about texting to let him know when she was leaving somewhere. Where she was going. When she arrived safely. Again, it had started as a joke but she'd done it. Without fail. Without question. Then he'd started not responding each time. So twice in the last few days she hadn't sent him the messages checking in.

It made her sick to her stomach, but she'd wanted to know if he'd really noticed her absence. He hadn't. He just…hadn't.

With a 24/7 dynamic such as theirs, trust and open communication were the only things that could keep it alive and thriving. Lately, she'd begun feeling a bit like a fraud.

Panic welled inside her but she tamped it down, burying the emotion as deep as she could.

She'd always thought they were on the same page. They had the same philosophies and desires. Other things she'd never discussed with him that made her feel special. Loved. Because she just assumed he knew how important they were. Writing them down made them real to her and so *he* was never far from her. Different colors of pen on a little folded piece of paper — they were like a shield to protect her.

Things he did seemingly automatically but she could look at on the paper and remember how amazing he was and how he loved her completely. And how she needed that attention. She'd grown to depend on it, and it scared her so much.

She turned the water off, shaking her head at the labyrinth of reasoning she'd thrown herself into. Getting dry didn't take long but she just didn't seem to be able to get warm. Taking out the clip in her hair, she tried to shake off the panic crawling through her body. She set the clip on the bathroom counter and killed the light.

She walked through the bedroom and went quickly downstairs to turn off the lights there too. She was certain Wes had locked the door but she checked, anyway. *Locked.*

One last light switch and the kitchen fell into darkness.

Passing the counter by the back door, she had to resist the urge to pull out their rules. That was what she'd always called them, but lately she'd started thinking of them as *her* rules. That made her sad, and another connection to them seemed to slip through her fingers.

If he'd just worked longer hours then she didn't think she'd feel so lost, but it was more than that. Much more. It seemed as if everything was changing. Everything.

Change wasn't bad, not in theory at least.

It didn't take her long to go up the stairs and into their bedroom. She crawled into bed and turned out the last lamp on her nightstand.

Michael reached over and pulled her into the safety of his body. He held her close, breathing in her hair. "Love you."

Tears threatened as she wrapped his arm tighter around her and snuggled against him beneath the covers.

She didn't know how to fix it yet. She couldn't even figure out how to broach the subject. But she'd figure it out. She had to. Or their marriage and everything they'd built was doomed to fail.

Chapter Four

Michael

Talk about being busy as fuck at work. Not a little bit here and there. More like a fuck ton of shit that just keeps piling on and on and…

With no end in sight, he couldn't have been happier. The business kept finding him, which made Michael feel as if he had balls the size of NYC.

That was what he got for breaking off and starting his own firm.

Little had he known that almost all of his clients would come with him. Several incredibly prolific clients, such as Wes.

If he'd known how successful he would be, he'd probably have left a year earlier.

Best part?

Being so busy.

Worst part?

Being so busy.

As always, he'd already spent several hours that morning out on two of his current construction sites. His crew chiefs were right on schedule, which kept the clients happy and coming back for more. Best guys he could have hired, hands down.

He almost felt bad for hiring them away from his former employer. Almost. But the guys seemed happier than he'd seen them in years. Himself included.

So busy was something he just had to manage.

Daily.

'Busy keeps you out of trouble, boy.' His father's voice preaching at him cropped up at the most inopportune times.

His father was a piece of work. A grade-A asshole with a side order of narcissistic prick. Unfortunately, he had also been a single dad. Michael's mom had died having him. Well, a couple weeks afterward, from complications. He'd always missed her, wondering what things could have been like if she'd been around.

He'd never asked if his dad blamed him for his mom's death. The answer had been incredibly easy to find all on his own.

Michael had always been thankful he didn't have any siblings. He wouldn't have wished his father on anyone else. Not even on a brother or sister to share the burden of being his legacy.

His earliest memory was of his old man smacking him on the back of the head when he'd handed him the wrong kind of screwdriver.

He'd been probably four at the time.

Bonding with his father had consisted of Michael being told to bring him another beer when he got home from working a double.

Nothing he did was good enough. Everything he attempted was stupid. Nothing ever met his father's approval. Except when he moved out. That, his father had said he appreciated, since he'd been tired of taking care of a freeloader. Him getting a scholarship to college, straight As, and working part-time in high school apparently hadn't been good enough.

'Drawing buildings and putting them up can be done by anybody. It won't get you anywhere.' Some days that endless loop played in his head and he pushed even harder to kick ass.

There was only one thing he'd gotten from his father that was worth anything—his work ethic. He got up early, stayed late and did the best job on everything he endeavored to accomplish.

Hopefully Michael wasn't a prick about it like his father, but he wanted to be a success. He wanted to make Tabitha proud, and build a firm he could pass down to their kids if they decided to have some.

His wife even helped him with the books when he needed it, but only when he asked. *Talk about a smart chick.* She did their taxes and invested extra, but they decided what to do together.

Always together.

Everything side by side.

He stood up from his desk and stretched his neck and shoulders. *Oy.* Too much sitting hunched over his drawing tablet for one morning. The civic center downtown was going to be incredible. He couldn't believe his luck in having been recommended for the project. A friend of his on the city council had apparently been talking him up. He looked intently at the blueprints on the screen he'd been working on for several days. *Almost done.*

He stared into his coffee cup and tried to remember if he'd eaten lunch. His stomach growled in response. "No food. Got it."

Unable to sit down again, he snagged his cup and headed to the small kitchen in the back. It was quiet inside the offices for once. He'd given everyone else the afternoon off, since they'd finished another huge project at Camp Lejeune the week prior. So, he'd told them all to go home and take it easy. He'd had every intention of just working a half day, too, but he had so much he needed to catch up on.

On the way to the kitchen there was a long hallway, lined with images of some of his projects. Each frame held two pictures — before and an after.

There wasn't much more satisfying than seeing what he'd built with his own hands. Staring at the walls and rooms around him gave him more fulfilment than he'd thought possible in a job. He'd built the location he stood in. He'd designed it as a showroom and workspace. He stepped into the kitchen and smiled looking at his hot dog steamer and popcorn machine. Every time he saw them they made him happy. Just like Tabitha.

Mmm…

Hottest wife ever.

He rinsed out his mug and grabbed a flavored water out of the fridge along with the stuff to make a sandwich. He polished off two sandwiches and a mini bag of chips before he slowed down.

After unscrewing the cap on his water, he drank deeply and closed his eyes with satisfaction.

That adage about loving a job will mean never working a day in your life? It couldn't have been more true.

Having a reputation to be proud of was worth a lot.

Word of mouth sending him winning bid after winning bid made his dick hard.

Getting to prove his dad wrong was priceless.

He actually hadn't even wanted to tell his father anything about the new company. There was only one time a year he called him, and it took some serious convincing from Tabitha to do even that.

His old man's birthday.

Michael had waited a couple years to make sure the company was going to do well, and it had more than tripled in profit from the first to second year, so he'd told him all about it.

The conversation had gone about how he'd expected.

A grunted hello, grousing about why he never called, snide remarks about not getting any younger. *Yeah. He was a real winner.*

Then Michael had dropped the bomb about Graves Design and Construction. Been going almost two years. Amazing. Profitable. Growing. Staff to help him. Supportive and beautiful wife. Amazing house. Amazing life. He was happy and wished he could be the same.

The guy had been speechless.

It was the first time probably in his whole life his father

seemed unable to think of anything to say.

Michael had laughed and wished him a happy birthday, then told him he had to go. His father had stammered a goodbye and that had been that.

If it hadn't been for Tabitha urging him to call, he never would have.

He'd never have had the satisfaction of proving him wrong. He didn't need the words that he was proud of him. Those words would never come and he was okay with that.

Why?

Because the only one who mattered was his wife.

His hot wife.

His property.

His submissive.

He headed to his office and sat back down, adjusting his cock beneath his slacks since he'd thought about his Tabby.

An ache settled inside him because he'd gone all morning and part of the afternoon without seeing her. He'd gotten up and showered and had been out before her alarm had gone off.

He missed the mornings he'd wake her up with his head between her thighs. Fuck, he loved her coming on his mouth to start the day. Or she sucked him off to get him out of bed. *Best. Alarm. Ever.*

The extra time they'd spent away from each other had been hard on both of them, but he knew she'd always be there for him. For them. And it was *for them* because everything he did he ran through the filter of making their lives better. Easier.

No man had loved a woman more than he loved Tabitha. None.

He glanced at his clock and checked his texts from Tabby. She'd asked him to come home for dinner by seven. That gave him five and a half more hours to work before he had to leave. For a date kind of dinner.

Hell, yes.

Her cooking? Out of this world good. If she didn't love

being a CPA so much he'd have suggested to her long ago to become a chef. She could open a restaurant in a city with a population of ten and make it a success.

They were even taking a cooking class together every Saturday.

Then there was their sex life.

Sex, off the charts kind of tasty.

Luckiest man ever.

Her being a hot wife? Fucking other men because he said she could? Having the control to take it away at any time? So delicious.

Sharing his favorite toy was deliciously dirty, but knowing she was still *his* toy? *Fuck.*

Nothing compared to it.

It pushed all of his buttons. Several buttons that he didn't even have names for. But he didn't have to explain them because Tabitha understood all of them.

She was perfect for him.

She'd been waiving their lines a bit lately. Nothing big enough for him to actually say anything about, but he'd definitely been aware of them. Her wearing panties around him or the timing of the other night with Wes? It hadn't been on the schedule as long as they'd agreed to.

Well…

He stared at the ceiling. At least he didn't think so, but he may have forgotten to check their calendar for a day…or two. *Ugh. Or a week.*

Not to mention being pretty certain he'd seen her in panties a few evenings before, but she was literally the most amazing creature on the planet.

Wanting to bring up tiny things like that…no thanks.

Especially not for the kind of *rules* they'd joked about for years.

The last person in the world he had to worry about was his purring Tabby.

His cock twitched behind his fly again. Her making that noise. Only for him.

Fuck.

He'd just had her two nights prior. Deep in her ass as Wes fucked her throat.

For a second, he closed his eyes and laced his hands behind his head.

Wes wasn't the only person they fooled around with, but he was on a very short list. There were less than a handful of men he would consider Tabitha's current hot wife dates.

Ares, a buddy from the gym he'd met a few years back. Bald, jacked. She'd said the first time he was with her he'd just ripped off her outfit, lifted her up and fucked her in the middle of the room. Not against the wall. Just standing with her thighs over his arms. She'd told Michael afterward she'd come twice before he put her down.

Duke, his best friend from back home in Kansas, had had the privilege a time or two when he'd flown over to see them for a weekend. The guy'd had a cocky attitude for days. The only thing he had more of was charm. He'd charmed his hands into Tabitha's panties beneath the table at a restaurant downtown within five minutes of being seated. It was now *their* booth at the little Italian restaurant, Bella Luna, thirty minutes outside the city. The booth with her cum all over it was most definitely his favorite. Duke had a trip planned to see them in a few weeks. Michael'd forgotten to tell Tabitha about it. *Forgotten. Sure. That was the word.* Could have been something about surprising her with a little bit of hot wife fun. Maybe some cuffs. A bit of Duke's whips. She creamed over being striped by his dragontail. Vicious toy. Yummy wife.

Hottest wife ever.

Each day he probably told her that a half a dozen times.

Not anywhere close to how many times he thought it, though.

Because she was.

The most amazing creature on the entire planet and she was his. He made plans to take her in the shower before bed.

He grinned.

And he'd take her again in bed before he fell asleep on her, inside her, beside her. All perfect.

Leaning forward, he glanced at the date.

Something about it kept poking him in the frontal cortex like he should remember. It wasn't her birthday, which was in the first part of December. It wasn't their anniversary, which was in the latter part of August.

He grabbed his phone to check their calendar to see if there was something in there when his desk phone lit up. He took a deep breath, silenced his cell, then traded it for the other phone and looked at the display.

Museum of the Marine.

Area code of Jacksonville.

He glanced at the clock and calculated time. He had hours left. Still plenty for what he needed to get done.

Pushing the talk button, he lifted the phone receiver to his ear. "Graves Design and Construction, this is Michael speaking. How can I help you?"

* * * *

Several hours later, he was so damn close to being done with the civic center plan. He'd kicked ass with the quiet of his office and only one phone interruption.

And he couldn't even call it an interruption.

The amazing opportunity had come from some of his work at the military base. Word of mouth had turned his business into a success.

Rubbing his eyes felt so good it made his dick hard.

How long had he—?

Oh. Fuck.

He dropped his hands and focused on the clock again.

He was already fifteen minutes late for his date with Tabitha. And it would take him at least forty-five minutes to get home with traffic, since he hadn't left in time.

"Dammit!" he barked at no one in particular.

He snatched up his phone and wondered if it had gone dead again. Talk about needing a new phone battery. The charge sucked and he just couldn't seem to remember to grab the extra charger from the house.

Pushing the wake-up button on the bottom row of buttons, Michael made the display light up.

Six texts from Tabitha.

"Fuck," he cursed again.

Silenced. He'd silenced the damn phone when the museum had called and he'd forgotten to turn it back on.

He hated nothing more than disappointing Tabitha. His stomach dropped as he pulled up her texts, which were all a few minutes apart.

You on your way, my husband?
Hello…
Knock knock.
Anybody home?
Did your phone die again?

Then at the bottom sat a picture of his wife's delicious cleavage. In an equally gorgeous, skin tight black dress.

Oh, my fucking hell that dress is incredible…BLIP. You make my heart stop.
I'm still at the office.
I'm so damn sorry. Got caught up in two projects.
Wish you would have called the office phone, even though I know you don't like doing that.
And now traffic is awful. Fuck.

He glanced at a monitor he had hanging in the corner of his office, which showed four different outdoor camera views along with twelve inside views.

I can see the 24 from here and it's completely packed.
I'm the worst husband ever. Forgive me? Please?
I promise to make it up to you when I get home…

47

As he waited his phone went dark and he brought their text screen up again.

Then he remembered all the notifications were still off. He'd muted his phone so he was distracted. He literally held his breath until he started to feel lightheaded.

He got into the settings and turned them on just in time for his phone to buzz in his hand.

He exhaled loudly when he got back to their screen.

There were a row of hearts and smiley faces.

Of course, I forgive you. I know how hard you're working.
Bet you're gonna be a while now, huh? The food I made probably isn't going to be awesome by the time you get here.

I feel like such an ass. So sorry, baby.

It's okay. I heard someone is going to make it up to me when he gets home.
I might have a few ideas for my husband…

Then a pic from up her skirt came through. *Skirt.* Michael wasn't certain if there was enough material to actually call it a skirt. And she most definitely didn't have panties on.

Hottest. Wife. Ever.
You're the best.
And that dress? Gonna look amazing beside the bed.
Be home as soon as I finish one thing and the traffic gets moving.
Love you, Tabby.

Love you!

Another row of rainbow hearts and kiss emojis came through.

He swiped the app to get it to disappear and checked the charge. *Dammit.* It wasn't gonna last until he got home. And he didn't have a charger with him.

Epic. Fail.

He moved his mouse to wake his computer up so he could dig back into work, get finished and get home to his lovely and forgiving wife.

Disappointing his wife had to be at the top of the shit pile of things to do. He hated it. But it wasn't just disappointment due to their dynamic. He was *more* to her, as she was *more* to him. Just…more. The connection went deeper, stronger.

People who had never experienced a kink relationship didn't know what they were missing. It fulfilled him in ways he'd never thought possible. But if he messed up it was as if he'd endured a physical blow.

The gut punch he was currently nursing was less than he deserved. He'd earned it by letting her down. She deserved a whole lot on top of his upset stomach to make up for it.

He needed to hire extra help, but to find people who could do what he did would take a hefty paycheck. Investing that money back into growing the business before hiring additional help would get them much more return in the long run.

"I'm doing this for us, baby. Only for us," he mumbled to his empty office. A yawn caught him off guard and his mouth split so far open his jaw cracked.

Long day.

He took a deep breath and tried to focus. He'd already been there twelve hours and exhaustion was beginning to catch up to him. There were only a couple things for the civic center plan he had to finish up and he could get the entire project sent off before he left. "An hour," he glanced at the clock with another yawn. "Maybe."

He pictured Tabitha wrapped up in a robe, reading a book or watching something on TV when he got home. *Fuck.* Maybe he could convince her to still be in that dress when he pulled in. He couldn't wait. *Mmm.* Sinking inside her tight heat before crashing sounded like the perfect way to end his long-ass day.

Even with all their combined baggage they'd come together and were some kind of perfect match. Like magnets or puzzle pieces, or cookies and milk. They helped each other be better.

And he'd never do anything to jeopardize that. Ever.

Even her being a hot wife and fucking other guys.

It wasn't for everybody, probably not most people, but for them, it worked and that was all that mattered.

He closed his eyes for a second and rubbed them.

An image of Tabitha wearing nothing but his collar flitted across his mind.

His collar.

Not something they'd agreed on. Not something they'd ever really talked about. He'd been thinking about it a lot lately, though.

His need to possess more of her had been growing.

He shook his head, staring at the screen. "Not now. Can't get lost in that right now. But soon and forever." He focused again, determined to get done quickly and get home to his girl.

"It will all be worth it with the bigger house we can buy, vacations we can take." He nodded, in full agreement with himself.

Epic. That was what he wanted her life to be. Epic.

Chapter Five

Tabitha

Standing next to the table, Tabitha cupped the top of a tapered candle and blew it out. She repeated the process two more times, dousing the once romantic dining room into a kiddie pool's worth of meh.

She moved back to her chair and exhaled one more breath that ruffled her bangs. It didn't take her two seconds of staring at the lovely dinner in front of her to completely deflate her 'everything is fine' attitude. She slumped back, wearing her new little black dress, and kicked her favorite heels off under the table.

After elbowing the arm of her chair, she propped her cheek on her fist.

It was fine. Truly.

In the scheme of things, it was such small potatoes she wouldn't even remember the slight in a few weeks.

Apparently, she could add lying to herself to her new bag of tricks.

"Ugh," she mumbled to the dinner getting cold in front of her.

She bit her bottom lip and gave herself permission to be upset for a few minutes.

So much for racing home after work to get dinner ready for date night.

And it was kind of their anniversary. Though not their wedding anniversary. If Michael had forgotten that she'd absolutely have known things were bad.

But they'd always celebrated the anniversary of the night

they met. They called it their meetversary. Five years before, they'd bumped into each other at a mixer get-together of his then-employer and her accounting firm.

Talk about electric.

Love at first sight was nothing but a figment of women's overactive imaginations around the world. Or so she'd thought.

She'd been walking around a corner and run right into him. Literally. He'd grabbed her before she fell. Like lightning, electricity had raced along her spine as he'd touched her.

For the first time in her life she'd been struck completely speechless by a man.

He'd eyed her mouth and she'd licked her lips.

The gesture hadn't been some kind of come on. She just hadn't been able to find her voice. Then he'd growled.

A dominant sound that had spoken directly to her soul.

Holy shit.

Sexiest man she'd ever seen.

Ever.

Eventually she'd fixed her momentary muteness and they'd introduced themselves. He'd bought her a drink, and asked for her number before they'd parted ways hours later.

The rest, as they say, was history.

But not some inconsequential history of people she'd never met.

No, it was their history. The start of their happily ever after.

One of their special moments they always celebrated, no matter how busy they were, so they could stop and remember those first words. First kiss. First…everything.

Tonight was listed in their shared calendar, the apps on their phones syncing up their lives and appointments and meetings and dates. Their dates and their *dates*.

Michael had never missed it before. Not till today.

One last *ugh* left her lips, then she stood to haul everything back into the kitchen.

Tabitha wanted to throw it all out, cause she definitely wasn't hungry anymore. She should eat, but eating alone always left her feeling worse than throwing it out. She could just put it in containers and heat it up for leftovers tomorrow but it would probably be gross. She shook her head. The seafood in the pasta would never keep with the sauce on it and she hated to waste good food.

A thought popped into her head as if it was a light switch flicking on. Before she lost her nerve, she grabbed the cordless house phone and dialed Robin, her best friend, a few houses down the road. She and her husband Roland had become neighbors after Tabitha and Michael had moved in and the couples were extremely close. Tabitha hadn't seen Robin all week and she honestly really needed a girl kind of powwow.

"Hello?"

"Have you had dinner yet?" Tabitha asked by way of hello.

"Does a package of Pop-Tarts count?"

Tabitha laughed, already knowing she'd called the right person to help her out of her funk. "Not if you're over the age of fourteen."

"Then no."

Staring at the counter, Tabitha pointed and listed things off. "I have linguini with scallops, salad with homemade croutons and cheesecake."

"I'm pretty sure I just drooled on the cat. What kind of cheesecake?"

"Turtle. Homemade. As if there's any other kind."

"I'll be at your door in less than forty-five seconds."

The phone clicked in Tabitha's ear and she smiled as she pushed the off button.

Robin was gorgeous. One of those chicks Tabitha wanted to hate but just couldn't. She was beautiful with her dirty blonde hair, colorful stripe and striking green eyes. Not to mention friendly, down-to-earth and fiercely loyal. Setting down the phone, she thanked her lucky stars they'd met the first weekend after she and Michael bought the house. Fate had definitely had a hand in them meeting.

Tabitha barely had time to dig her heels out from under the table and swap them out upstairs for her fuzzy caterpillar slippers before the doorbell chimed throughout the house.

Opening the door, Tabitha stepped aside to let Robin in. "You weren't kidding when you said less than a minute. I almost didn't have time to get my slippers."

Robin pulled her close and hugged her tightly. "And let that be a lesson to you when you call mentioning scallops and cheesecake."

Tabitha motioned her in and shut the door behind her. "You know the way." She turned back around and Robin was eyeing her from head to toe.

"I know neither of our doors swing toward the girl-on-girl action side of things, so why the LBD?" Her gaze went to Tabitha's feet and she grinned. "And caterpillars?"

Tabitha thought of several things to say, a couple of lies and a couple of half-truths. "Ugh," came out instead.

"Oh, goodness. This sounds like quite a story. Good thing I came hungry."

Tabitha took her elbow and they moved toward the kitchen. "Very good thing. Everything almost ended up in the trash."

"Blasphemer," she gasped and actually made the sign of the cross before looking at the ceiling. "She didn't mean it, Honoré."

Handing over a plate when they got to the kitchen, Tabitha raised an eyebrow. "Honoré?"

"Patron saint of desserts or something like that. Can't be too careful you know." Robin stared at the food and did a little dance. "My Pop-Tarts can suck it."

They both made plates and sat down at the breakfast nook table off to one side of the kitchen. The last thing Tabitha wanted to do was sit in the depressing dining room.

"Who cancelled? Michael or a date?"

"Michael," Tabitha confessed and her stomach tightened with unease. Saying it out loud made it sound far too real.

Robin was a hot wife, too. The kink relationship her and her husband had was different from what Tabitha shared with Michael, but the hot wife dynamic they had in common had made them inseparable almost at the first hi-how-are-ya.

They'd found it out kind of by accident at a weekend block party several years before, right after they'd moved in. Being two of the only households in the neighborhood with no children, they'd gravitated toward each other and had had a connection from the word go. One conversation had led into another and one of them had revealed they were a hot wife. There had definitely been alcohol involved. They hadn't scarred any of the neighborhood kids. Well… not permanently.

"Oh. Well. Shitballs. I was hoping it was one of the others and then you could just kick them to the curb. Lots more out there who want a piece of what we have to offer. But Michael letting you down definitely isn't a good thing. First time?"

Tabitha just stared at her for a long second then glared at the food on her plate so she could successfully push it around the circular porcelain in front of her. "I keep expecting things to settle back into our routine."

"But?" Robin prompted as she dug into her food.

Tabitha tried to order her thoughts as if they were a math equation. "But now I'm starting to think what's been happening lately is becoming the new norm and I'm a bit at a loss as to how I want to handle it."

"You know I'm not going to judge and you know I'll keep everything to myself if you want to talk about it. And that includes from Roland. He knows us girls have to *blah, blah, blah* stuff out to another girl sometimes just to hear how it sounds outside our own heads."

"I do."

"And you also know I'll make witty banter at you for

forty minutes if you don't want to talk about it, right?"

Tabitha smiled. "I know that, too. You wouldn't risk the cheesecake."

"Hell, no, I wouldn't. I can already taste it." She took another bite of linguine. "So, are we talking or are we *talking*?"

It took Tabitha a second to decide. "*Talking,* I think, which calls for wine."

"Totally. But just a glass since I don't have a designated walker to get me home."

Tabitha got up and grabbed glasses and a bottle of white to complement the pasta. "I'll make sure you get home safe. I'm sure Roland would come down to get you if we called him."

"Not home. He's away on a business trip and comes back tomorrow. I can't wait, either. I only sleep well when he's pressed up against me in bed."

"Completely agree," Tabitha added as she poured the wine.

Robin held her glass up and waited for Tabitha to follow suit. "To the hottest wives on the block. May we always have the most interesting lives on our street."

"And on our backs." Tabitha smiled and took a drink.

"Such a dirty girl. I'll drink to that!"

Tabitha contemplated how lucky they were when they met. "You know, I think it's some kind of fate we live close to each other. It's not like there are hot wife support groups out there or meetings we could attend."

"We should totally start one. How freakin' funny would that be? We could even have themed snack food. People would just die over it."

Tabitha could see the wheels in Robin's head working. "I almost hate to ask, but...themed food?"

"Like little sausages, for obvious reasons." She bobbed her eyebrows and took another drink of wine. "Cum punch made of ginger ale and sherbet. Epic." Shrugging, she continued, "I've talked to some people online but, yeah. Not awesome from what I've found. So, I completely agree with the fate assessment. People are brought into our lives for a reason. Some good and some bad, but you are definitely in the good egg category. As in the best, for reasons that are not on the agenda to talk about tonight. Okay, lay it on me. What's Michael doing or not doing—or is it more than one specific thing?"

"Can I ask a question first?"

"Of course. Shoot."

"Do you and Roland have rules when it comes to you sleeping with other guys?" Tabitha hadn't asked her before. Too personal before tonight, maybe.

"Sure. I think most of us do. Some only have a few things and others have pretty elaborate setups, I would imagine. One thing I think we all have in place is some kind of power exchange to start with, so we all feel safe." She made air quotes with her fingers for the last two words. "Someone has to be in charge. Which partner was in charge could be different. Plus how balanced or unbalanced the dynamic is, I'm sure, widely different. One person makes all the decisions, or they share them more equally. One person creates all the rules and they both follow them, or it's some kind of happy medium. It's all about what makes everyone feel comfy in the situation. Physically or otherwise."

Tabitha nodded. "Exactly. We have certain things we've always gone by. Parameters, I guess, that made both of us comfortable to jump in the deep end. Around a handful of things that have been my guidelines to stay within so everything is nothing but fun."

"Sounds great."

"But I've been pushing against them lately."

"Oy. Not so great. Anything really hcinous?"

"Absolutely not. I would never do anything to violate Michael's trust in me. That makes me want to vomit just thinking it. No, I'm more brushing up against our lines. Testing them, but not in a mean or vindictive way."

"Testing them. Interesting choice of words." Robin stared

at her for a second or two. "Testing the rules or testing your relationship? Two very different things."

Tabitha moved her plate away, giving up the farce of actually eating. She just wasn't hungry. "I wasn't consciously testing us or him, but it's sort of turned into something like that. That makes me sound awful."

"No, it doesn't. Concerned, maybe, but not awful. You've been pushing your food around and there's definitely something going on between you two. What is testing the boundaries all about? Why did you start? Something must have kicked it off."

"Michael had been distracted for a few weeks. Every morning he left early, texting during the day was minimal, late getting home, obviously exhausted so he wasn't awake long before crashing. I was missing him so I started putting little things in our calendar app we have on our phones. Little messages to make him laugh because the first thing he did every morning was check our calendar. I was so excited the next morning, waiting for him to text or call or add something back. This wasn't the first time I did it so it wasn't a brand-new concept. Then that morning turned into afternoon and nothing. Next day, same thing. I finally asked about it and he apologized, said he was just so busy and he forgot to check our calendar for a few days."

"That's less awesome."

"Tell me about it. Things that I'd come to count on for our connection don't seem to be a priority for him anymore."

"Did things get better?"

"Yeah. For a little bit. But I check every once in a while and put something odd in there. Like we're going to learn how to take care of baby bats on Thursday."

"Anything?" Robin asked, sounding hopeful.

Tabitha just shook her head. "When stuff comes up and he misses things it makes me feel less important. But I know how busy he is. I know how many extra hours he's putting in because of so much business. That's not something I want to crap on in any way. We're so lucky that his company has kicked ass when so many others are struggling. And the thought that I'm being needy is just awful. Submissive is decadent and sexy. Needy? Hell to the no."

"I get that, but have you talked to him about it?"

"About the calendar stuff? A couple times."

"I'm assuming there is more going on? More than just him missing a few things you're flirting with him over an app."

"A few other things are just…different. Completely not how we've had them in the past. But one is the worst."

"What?"

"I need a strong reconnection after a date. It's like coming…"

"Home?" Robin offered.

Tabitha blew out a breath she'd been holding. "Exactly. And lately it's been off. Not completely missing. Also, not what we've done in the past. But things can change, and I realize that."

"Changing is inevitable, I agree. But you guys have to change together. In the same direction, especially with what we are. Anything else won't work."

"Agreed."

"So…" Robin was blunt to a fault, so Tabitha was worried when she didn't continue.

"What?"

"Trying to think of a nicer way to ask this, but I'm coming up short."

"Just ask it. I'm sure I've already asked myself the same question."

"Do you think he's cheating?"

And there it was. It was like a flashbang tossed into the room, but Tabitha was right. She had already thought of it. "No. Not at all."

"What makes you so certain? Happens all the time in this lifestyle."

"It's just not him. Not how he's wired. He's a monogamous kind of guy. Possessive. And he would never violate our relationship like that. He's messed up a lot lately, but that's just not something I have to worry about."

"Positive?" she asked with raised eyebrows.

"One hundred percent."

"I love that you're so sure. That's actually really awesome."

"It is. But it's also what's made it so hard to bring it all up."

"How so?"

"He's not doing anything horrible. He's not cheating. Not breaking our vows. Not lying. Just missing stuff." Tabitha closed her eyes for a second. "Something else that's different lately is our kink dynamic."

"I need cheesecake if we're going to talk kink or I'm going to probably end up humping your couch. With Roland being gone I'm going a bit stir-crazy when it comes to sex. One of our rules is I can't play if he's out of town. So. Damn. Horny."

Tabitha got up and carried her dirty dishes to the sink. Robin followed with hers. "How long's he been gone?"

"All week. I'm going to attack him when he walks in the door."

"Welcome-home sex is awesome." Tabitha grabbed what they needed for dessert and headed back to the table.

"Sex is awesome."

"Hear, hear," Tabitha toasted and finished her glass of wine.

"I've got a random question for you before I pick your brain a bit more on the situation."

"Shoot."

"What kind of salad dressing was that?" Robin asked, pointing to the bottle on the counter.

"Thousand island."

"I've had that before but it wasn't nearly as good. Yours was awesome. Where'd you get it?"

"I made it."

"You're shitting me."

Tabitha snickered as she handed over a plate of dessert. "*That* is definitely not a fetish of mine."

Robin took a bite. "Mmm…" She groaned and licked off another spoonful. "Where did you learn to cook like this? You're really good, Tabby. Like…good. I just don't have a knack for it."

"Anyone can learn. I've cooked all my life. Just enjoy it. Michael and I are actually taking a class down at the community college. Great instructor, a few hours on the weekend. We have a blast. If you're really interested, I'll get you the info. Bet you'd really delight in it."

"I can't cook. You know this. Need I bring up the salad incident?"

"Oh, please, no. That was awful. But a great reason to take a cooking class."

Skepticism rolled off Robin as she finished her cheesecake. "Okay. I can function again. Kink dynamic. What's different? And then I have another question."

Tabitha opted for another glass of wine. "I have more of a dynamic right now with Wes than I do with Michael. I really like our sexual relationship. Love how rough he is, how dominant. But that's normally more along the lines of what I have with Michael. Not the really rough stuff because Michael and I just don't play like that anymore, but the rest of it? The control and the possession… I miss it. But our dynamic, mine with Michael, is there all the time. Sometimes boiling and sometimes just on a simmer, but it's always there."

"Which means Wes is probably the one you're seeking out lately? As opposed to maybe Ares from the gym a few weeks back?"

Another sip of wine made heat fill Tabitha's cheeks. Of course, it was the wine, and not that Robin had hit the nail on the head so easily. "Correct. Did you get a degree in closet therapy I didn't know about?"

"Hell, no. Not enough money in the world to deal with crazy people all the time." Robin rubbed her fingers along her lips. "Do you think that's why Michael approves of you doing more things with Wes? Why he gives you more latitude with him? Because he's vicariously getting you what you need, even if he's not the one supplying your fix?"

"I've thought about it. Didn't much like the concept of him passing me off to someone else to care for. I can't imagine him making a *conscious* decision on his part to do that. But subconsciously?" She didn't answer the question. Didn't want to. Not out loud. Especially not after a super long day, when she still felt more than a bit off from him missing dinner. Instead of talking about that anymore, she decided to change the subject. *Hopefully.* "Your other question?"

"I didn't think you guys did dates at the house. Did that change? I was coming home the other night and saw Wes walking out of the house. He looked…satisfied." Robin bobbed her eyebrows at her.

"We don't normally do it, but it's not exactly a rule. Wes is the only one who's been here. Mostly for business stuff. And then for some extracurricular activities, as well. He's a good guy we've known for a while and we trust him. The date all together wasn't something that was a huge plan. That's happening this Saturday. But Michael had been so preoccupied and I'll admit to being ridiculously horny. He said to plan what I wanted and it was fine by him. He'd be home around nine and would take care of me after Wes used me."

"Damn."

"I know. Delicious. So, I left Wes a message on his cell. Might have been a bit dirty."

"Sounds deliciously hot, but…" One of Robin's brows lifted and she waited.

"But… Exactly. I don't fuck other guys just to fuck them. It's something that brings us pleasure. Michael and I. I don't ever want it to be about what I want. Or just me having fun."

"*Blech.* I know exactly what you mean. It's the same for me. That holds no appeal to me at all. That's an open relationship. Which I want nothing to do with. You?" Robin asked.

"Me neither. It's about us or it's a no-go from me. And not fully reconnecting isn't working for me. It makes me feel lost."

Robin reached across the table and squeezed her hand. "You already know what you need to do. You need to talk to him and address all of your issues. And quick. Letting these kinds of things fester in our world, in this dynamic, does not work. Trust me. Been there, done that I-am-an-island routine. Or a martyr. Played that one, too. Never would have stayed married to Roland if we hadn't worked it all out years ago." She held up her hands momentarily. "We're not perfect by any means, but we're also both pretty vocal if something is wrong. You have to be."

Tabitha held up two fingers and appreciated the wine giving her a little extra courage to say more than she normally would. "Two things. I don't like to make waves, especially when everything could fall back into our normal routine and I could have avoided all the extra worry and negative feelings of bringing everything up I'm worried about."

"And what's the second thing?"

"Talking about my feelings makes me want to vomit."

"Ha!" Robin laughed and stood, grabbing things to put away. "Ick. I know, awful in the best-case scenario, but it's no good to be miserable all the time with worry and negative feelings that you're having regardless, and when you don't talk it will probably perpetuate the rollercoaster of badness. It's better to just yank off the bandage quick so you can get to the bottom of things and get back on the same track."

Tabitha stood and started putting things in the fridge. "I hear you saying the right stuff. I know that's exactly what I'm supposed to do."

"But?" Robin asked with a cock of her hip and a raised eyebrow.

"Getting disappointed in Michael seems more harsh. Maybe because of the dynamic. Maybe just because I'm emotional and a bit scared. I know I don't wear his collar. It's just not something we ever did." Another kind of disappointment crept inside and Tabitha shoved it down deep.

Adding more to her pile of not-great at the moment wasn't a good idea.

It didn't matter that he'd never wanted to own her like that.

It didn't. At all.

She took a breath and tried to refocus on Robin, who wore a sympathetic expression. "But our connection is that strong, I think. So, the tentative disconnection from him at any time is…terrifying."

Robin grabbed her hand for a second and gave it a squeeze. "I know exactly how you feel. It's so scary."

"Why is it so easy to talk to you about it? I've made my points rationally and all is good. But the thought of talking to Michael about it? I could run a half marathon with all the adrenaline racing through my system. Plus, we have a date planned with Wes for the weekend and I want to see how it goes after that. It could go amazingly well and everything gets back on track. Right?"

"Things aren't going to magically fix themselves. Especially if Michael doesn't even know there's a problem. And trust me, he doesn't know. He's a dude."

"I just don't want to rock the boat when he's so very busy. And so very happy." Tabitha shrugged and headed to the fridge with a couple containers to put away. "I'll figure it out from this weekend and go from there."

Robin shook her head and handed her the last container. "I want it on the record that I think that's a bad idea. I think you need to talk to him first."

"Duly noted. I've already set the day for our next date which was supposed to be happening here, but after yesterday, I really don't think I want to do that. I liked the hot factor."

"Wicked dirty."

"But having someone else in our bed just doesn't do it for me. Not right now."

"Understandable."

"And if I change it to a hotel then we could have neutral space to talk if things do go as planned."

"Now you're talking."

The whirl of the motor on the garage door opener came to life and Tabitha smiled.

"I love seeing you so happy when he comes home." Robin took her hand and squeezed it. "Even with everything else happening, as long as you still have that, then the rest is just details."

A door opened and closed. "Tabitha?" Michael called out for her.

"In the kitchen with Robin."

He came around the corner, loosening his tie, and grinned at them. He glanced at their clasped hands. "Is there something I don't know about you two?" Pulling Tabitha close, he kissed her lips and went back for seconds. "Damn, you look gorgeous in that dress. So sorry I missed dinner." He kissed her again.

"Hey now," Robin chastised. "Don't damage the merchandise. I'm trying to steal her away from you. I could keep her as my slave for fettucine and cheesecake."

They all laughed.

"I'm gonna get out of your hair," Robin announced. "The wine is catching up with me, anyways."

Michael yawned and shook his head. "Don't let me run you off. I need to shower."

"You hungry?" Tabitha asked. "We just finished putting stuff away. I could heat something up for you?"

He yawned again and shook his head. Bet he thought that would get rid of the exhaustion climbing all over him. It was how he came home most nights after leaving the house at five. "Naw. I grabbed a sandwich after I texted you. Not super hungry."

"I'll walk Robin home so I can see what she has to offer on

the slave opportunity and then I'll be right back."

"The perks are going to be legion," Robin added.

"We'll see about that," Tabitha challenged.

"Sounds great to me," Michael mumbled as he trudged up the stairs.

Tabitha wondered if he really had any idea what he'd just encouraged.

When he was out of earshot Robin turned to her. "I see what you mean with the exhaustion. Poor guy looked dead on his feet."

"Exactly." They headed out of the front door and continued to the sidewalk. Darkness had fully descended but thankfully it was still warm so Tabitha wasn't chilly in her dress. And slippers. "Which makes it harder to find a moment I want to waste talking about this when the time we have together is such a precious commodity."

At Robin's front door, they paused and Tabitha gave her a big hug. "Thanks for tonight. I needed it."

"Anytime," Robin told her. "And I still think you need to talk to him. Have to start somewhere, you know? Make it simple. If you don't freak out, then he won't freak out. Easy-peasy."

It was the truth. The wine she'd downed spoke up and told her to be brave. "Maybe I will when I go back. It doesn't have to be some huge meeting or anything like that."

"Exactly. Just bring it up and go from there. You want more time with him, and if you're not going to be my slave then I think he's a great catch."

Tabitha laughed as she headed back down Robin's steps. Halfway down she stopped and turned around.

"What? Are you gonna be my slave?" Robin clapped her hands and did a little dance.

"No."

"Dammit."

"I'll do you one better. You free on Saturday?"

"In the morning, I am. Roland is supposed to be home sometime in the afternoon."

"Perfect. I'll get you the details." Tabitha turned to go.

"The details on what?" Robin called after her.

"It's a surprise, but you'll love it."

"Why do I have the distinct impression I should ask a lot more questions about this?"

"Bye." Tabitha waved and drew a halo around her head.

"Oh…Lord," were the only two words Tabitha could make out before she started laughing again.

Tabitha hurried back down the sidewalk past a few houses to get back to hers. She went inside, locked the door, turned everything off downstairs then went up, determined to talk to her husband. Being a chickenshit about talking to him wasn't going to get her anywhere.

"Micha—" His name died on her lips as she walked into the bedroom.

He was completely naked…and out cold on the bed. It looked as if he'd made it into the shower and that was it.

Tabitha shook her head and stripped off her dress.

She got ready for bed and climbed in next to him.

Automatically, he pulled her close and hummed against her shoulder before falling back asleep.

Closing her eyes, she relaxed into him.

Everything would be fine and she'd talk to him in the morning before he took off for work.

Maybe.

Chapter Six

Tabitha

Friday night.

Six o'clock on a Friday night and she was home alone reading a book.

Meh.

Rereading the same page for the third or fourth time signaled that she needed a change of scenery.

Maybe she could find a new crochet project. *Meh*, again. Restlessness made her shift her legs beneath her.

After snapping the book closed, she tossed it on the end table next to her and stared through the living room into the open kitchen.

She'd been home for over an hour.

Michael had already texted and said he was going to be late. He'd sent a selfie of his head back, mouth hanging open and a snoring emoji. She'd smiled despite her restlessness.

Having stopped on the way home at the grocery store, she knew what was in the fridge. Stuff to make ribs and potato salad.

Glancing outside, she caught sight of the thermometer. Seventy-three degrees. Perfect to grill on the porch.

For one.

Meh squared.

Hauling herself out of the oversized comfy chair in the corner, she trudged toward the kitchen in her caterpillar slippers.

Cut-offs and a tank after work felt more than a little bit awesome. She wrapped her hair up, grabbed a clip off the counter and secured it in place.

She just needed to do something to get her mind off… things.

Yes.

That was exactly what she needed.

In the corner sat a CD player and she popped something in and turned it on. Loud.

Music filled the kitchen and she took a deep breath, and another one.

Everything was going to be great. All of the issues would get worked out as soon as she found the spine to tell Michael there was a problem.

They could fix anything together. Anything.

Maybe even tonight.

Passing by the stove, Tabitha noticed the clock read five after six. If he was home in the next couple hours, they might even have a chance to talk tonight. It could all be over in the morning.

She took another deep breath.

That would be so great. Worrying— one thing she didn't excel at. It tore her up and she was more than ready to be done with it.

Other than the actual emotional conversation, she was totally on board with the plan.

Sorta.

Grabbing everything she needed to boil potatoes, she carried them to the counter, then picked up one of the largest russets and a peeler. She'd tried just baking them and cutting them up but they came out too dry. Asking her chef instructor had given her a different method to try, so she figured she'd give it a go. Singing along to the music as she peeled, the worries and disappointments of the week melted away a bit. Not completely. But it was better than it had been in a while.

A squeak from the laundry room made her pause.

She jumped when the door to the garage opened.

"Honey, I'm home." Michael stepped into the kitchen,

holding his tie in one hand and a bottle of their favorite wine in the other.

For two seconds, maybe three, Tabitha stood there with a half-peeled potato in her hand as she stared at her husband. The music blared through the little player and Michael turned down the volume a bit.

"You're home early." Excitement filled her. "I thought you said you were going to be late."

"Surprise," he added with the decadent grin that always made her heart flutter in her chest. "Happy Meetversary, take two!"

No idea who moved first.

Michael put the wine on the counter and threw his tie next to it.

Tabitha chucked the potato and peeler on the counter.

They met in the middle.

Their lips collided and Michael picked her up. She wrapped her arms and legs around him and held on tight.

Tears welled, so she squeezed her lids and laughed against his mouth.

He turned his head and stared at her. "Are those happy tears, my wife?"

"The happiest," she mumbled and pulled him near again for another kiss.

Drawing away, he looked into her eyes again. "I love you emotional for me. For us. Love that it overwhelms you. Best feeling ever."

Tugging him closer, she mumbled, "More kissing from you. Less blubbering from me."

His chest shook as he chuckled and claimed her mouth again.

His mouth. Stuff fantasies were made of.

His hands? Wet dreams in the making.

He palmed her ass and held her tight. Tight enough she would wear his marks for several hours if she was lucky. A shiver ran up her back at the mere notion of his marks on her. More of that would be highly delectable.

Tabitha tasted his mouth as if it were for the first time. "You taste delicious."

"Ditto." He peeked over her shoulder. "Whatcha makin'?"

"Potato salad."

"With boiled eggs? And pickles? And mayo? And it's still warm? And mmm...bacon?" His eyes lit up and she laughed.

"Of course. I know what you like."

"Mmm. Yes, I do believe you do." He eyed her cleavage and her nipples peaked as he stared at them. "Point proven. Let me go upstairs and change and I'll come back down and help. Then we can eat together and maybe watch a movie or something. Sound like a plan? It'll be like our date last night, but I have my head out of my ass now."

"Sounds incredible."

He pressed his lips to hers one more time as he slowly released her body.

Sliding down his hard length reminded her of how thankful she was to have him. To be as attracted to him after five years of marriage made her so happy.

"Be right back." One more peck on the mouth and he snatched his tie off the counter and bolted up the stairs.

Tabitha wondered if he was really there or if he was a figment of her imagination and nothing more. Glancing at the counter, she stared at the Pinot Noir they loved from a small winery in Vienna.

Reaching for it, electricity zapped up her arm as her fingertips collided with the chilled glass.

Real. He was actually real. And he was home on time to have a do-over on their date.

A smile stretched her lips and she hoped her face froze like that. She shouldn't have been worried at all,

And she was so glad she hadn't said anything because he'd done tonight on his own and out of the blue.

It didn't take her half a minute to uncork the wine and pour half glasses for both of them.

Yes, she did use their fluted wedding glasses.

And do a little dance when she heard Michael moving around upstairs.

Ecstatic joy bubbled inside her when Michael came down the stairs and his eyes lit up when he saw the glasses. "I remember those. One of the happiest days of my life. Truly."

Tabitha handed him his glass and eyed him up and down. Tank top, cargo shorts, bare feet. *Damn.* Comfortable at home. Nothing better. It took her a minute to focus. Cause... *damn.* "One of the happiest?"

Holding up his glass, he waited for her to ting the glasses together. "Mm-hmm." His gaze held hers as he tasted the wine.

Raising the glass to her lips, Tabitha swirled the delicious flavors on her tongue. Perfection. Sweet, smooth, dry. Exactly why it was their favorite. "And what days have you been happier, my husband?"

"Every day since." His eyes deepened in color as he stared at her, and there wasn't laughter swimming in their depths. No. Just love. Unending love. Sincerity shone forth as he leaned forward for another kiss.

"You completely wreck me when you say things like that."

He set his wine glass on the counter. "Good. Love wrecking you. So much. Okay, El Capitan, put me to work. What do you need me to do?"

That was another thing she adored about her husband. Even though they truly had a 24/7 dynamic, he didn't use that as an excuse to shirk his duties to her as a husband or a partner. They did everything together. Cleaning, cooking, gardening.

They were a team.

An amazing one.

Tabitha took another sip of the wine that had already begun to relax her muscles and lessen the tension headache lurking behind her eyes. "I'm all over the potato salad, if you'll get the ribs ready for the grill. No need to turn the grill on yet, though, since I still have to cook the potatoes."

"Want me to boil the ribs first or just grill them?"

"You're the official meat man now. Up to you."

"You got it." He turned toward the fridge with a grin.

Setting her glass down, she tried to process her good fortune as she picked up her discarded potato and got back to peeling. "I have no idea how you got enough stuff done to leave early tonight, but whatever you did, I'm soooooo happy."

"Me, too. I hated disappointing you last night. Hated it. A lot. So, I worked through lunch and told another client his project would be delayed a day or two." He moved things around in the fridge to get to the packages of ribs. He went about his task as if what he'd said was no big thing.

"You did?" Talk about melt her insides.

"I most certainly did. Mmm. Meat."

"Hold on. Wait. Does that mean you think you're going to get more than your share of the ribs because you didn't eat lunch? Cause if you do, then you've got another think coming, mister." Tabitha washed off her potato and grabbed another.

"But I'm hungry. Wasting away, even. Don't you feel bad for me and want to give up your ribs?" His stomach growled as if to back him up. "See. Wasting away."

"You can have half an extra rib."

"What?" he groused in mock outrage as he picked spices. "I should get several extra from our sheer size difference alone."

Tabitha stared at the ceiling in concentration. "All right. One extra rib. Final offer."

"Final offer. You drive a hard bargain, ma'am. Sold."

"But I get more of the potato salad." She grinned as he acted offended.

"Brutal," he told her with a shake of his head. After grabbing the rest of the things he needed, he moved next to her on the counter.

Shoulder to shoulder making dinner together.

Fuck.

She'd had no clue how much she'd really missed him being home to do the domestic stuff together until he was back beside her. A huge amount didn't even scratch the surface. Leaning against his shoulder, she took a deep breath. "You smell good," she hummed as she breathed out.

He kissed her head and inhaled. "Damn. You, too. Love how you put perfume in your hair."

"Don't give away my trade secrets."

"Your secrets are safe with me."

And they were. Anything and everything she'd told him was safe with him. Even the hard stuff.

She chewed on the inside of her cheek and tried to think of how she could bring up what had been going on in her head lately.

"So, how was your day?" he asked as he flipped the top open on the barbeque spice.

Later.

She'd figure out how to talk to him about the bad stuff later.

Tonight was for them.

"Good. Busy as always. The franchise tax deadline is fast approaching and of course everyone waited until the last minute."

"Naturally. Which is why I keep my CPA on speed dial. She helps me with all of my financial planning."

"She does, does she? I'm pretty sure she had all of your taxes filed the first day it was open to file. Pretty sure she did that for you. At no extra charge."

He faced her with a wicked glint in his eye. "Hmm. I think you're right. Maybe some kind of bonus should *come* her way."

"I'm sure whatever you think suits her level of customer *service* would be greatly appreciated by all parties."

"Duly noted. After dinner, we should watch a movie and I'll offer my thanks as I see fit."

"How...intriguing." She laughed and tossed her potato skins in the trash. "And what about your day, my husband?

Anything new show up on your horizon?"

"Actually, two projects. Another military base project that I had an inkling about the other day from an email I received. But the second project kind of sprang up out of nowhere, and is going to be incredible."

The way he lit up talking about what he did every day delighted her. Seeing him happy was incredible. It fed her soul. Especially after he'd lost his love for creating at his former firm.

"What is it?" Tabitha bounced across the kitchen to grab a cutting board and one of her knives with the rainbow handle out of the block.

"Grab me a knife, too. Meat just has to rest till we're ready to cook now. I'll help you chop."

Grabbing a second knife, she got them all set to start cubing the potatoes. "So, what's the project? The one you were telling me about in Jacksonville?"

"No, actually. It's another high-profile job for a museum in Beaufort."

"Oh, I love that place." Beaufort was a beautiful town an hour to the east on the coast. "Which museum? Didn't think they had much by way of art there."

"It's the military museum. They need a new building put up and one of the higher-ups at Camp Lejeune is a benefactor over there and recommended me. They're actually the ones I talked to yesterday, and I got completely wrapped up in what they needed. It's gonna be an amazing property. I put a lot together today for what they wanted and sent them the preliminary contract. It was already signed and back in my hands before I left at six."

"Talk about being ready to roll."

"I know. No one's ever that on the ball, but it's privately owned by two brothers and they pretty much knew what they wanted. I'll have to meet with them next week, which will be tough, but we'll figure it out."

"Why tough?" They finished chopping and Tabitha got the potatoes cooking set another pot with eggs in to boil.

She set a timer and faced Michael, who was leaning against the counter with his arms crossed at his chest.

So hot.

"They are unbelievably busy during the week with all the other projects they have going on. We already compared schedules and it didn't go well. I'm only free in the afternoons between other projects and the construction finalizing on the new high school next week. They're only free in the mornings because they have some kind of fundraiser planning committee meeting every night next week. We'll work it out. It's worth it. Super awesome project."

"That's so great. I love you happy."

"And this part of the project is pretty small scale. They already said if it goes well, they have two other projects that will swiftly follow."

Stepping closer to him, she sighed when he automatically wrapped his arms around her. "You're such a rockstar."

"Just trying to keep up with my wife."

"Sweet talker."

"Every chance I get." He glanced around her and she followed his gaze to the food cooking on the stove. "What else do we need to do?"

"Cut up bread and butter pickles, and timewise I think we're pretty good to get the grill on and get crackin' on those ribs."

He pulled her close for a kiss. "I'll go turn on the gas, then. Fuck, I love talking to you."

"I love doing everything with you." Not a joke. Not an exaggeration. Each little thing she got to do was better with him.

"Wrecked." One more kiss and he pulled away to walk toward the back door.

Best unexpected Friday she could remember.

Walking to the fridge, she renewed her vow to make the most of their time together. Maybe this was the beginning of everything getting back on track. And she sure wasn't going to take it for granted.

* * * *

An hour and a half later, they were seated outside at the table on the patio, next to their garden, digging into dinner, and they were both on their second glass of wine.

Tabitha had forgotten she'd bought corn on the cob for the weekend so they'd shucked it waiting for the grill to heat and the potatoes to cook. Michael had buttered them up with salt and pepper and wrapped them in foil to put on the grill with the ribs.

Michael had been telling her all about his projects, and there were a lot of them to talk about. Him coming home early to have a surprise date with her was even that much more special with everything he had on his plate. The design work was legion and all of the construction crews he headed at the same time? *Yowza.*

"You do as much work as three regular people," Tabitha told him.

"It's a lot, but I don't think it's that much." He took a drink of wine. "At least not on some days. Next week is probably going to be a bit busier than normal."

Tabitha moved a rib to his plate.

"You do love me," he told her as he picked it up and gnawed on it. "Delicious."

After another bite of potato salad, Tabitha asked, "How much busier than normal?"

"Have to find time for the museum guys to come in and talk. Still don't know when that's going to happen. No matter how many times I try to shift things around the pieces don't fit yet. But I also have another big meeting with Wes and his project manager for that new government project."

"Well, I see it as very simple."

He paused mid-bite. "How's that?"

"Go in tomorrow and get some things done. You came home early tonight, which I'm sure put you even farther behind. Go take care of some of it so you aren't so stressed."

77

"But tomorrow's Saturday."

"Yes. So?"

"It's our cooking class."

Warmth and love filled her chest that he'd remembered. "Actually, I wanted to talk to you about that, too. Ask a favor. I was wondering if you'd mind if I took Robin with me. She can't boil water and I think Logan could maybe help. Maybe." She made a face and he laughed. "If you'd be okay with me taking her and broadening her horizons, then I'd say it would be a perfect opportunity for you to get some things marked off your ever-growing to-do list."

He pulled her close and kissed her mouth. His lips tasted like barbeque sauce and love.

"Like that idea, I take it?"

"Best. Wife. Ever. As in, the history of ever. That would be perfect." He stared at her very seriously. "But only if you're okay with me not going. Only if it's completely one hundred percent not going to upset you."

"I think it's perfect. I'd been meaning to talk to you about the cooking class since last night." She thought about it for a second. "And I'm totally okay with it. You'd actually be doing me a huge favor." Her gaze dropped to his crotch. "I might even owe you one in thanks."

"Oh, well, far be it from me to say no to a lady when she wants to say thank you." He gave her another kiss and they went back to eating.

Then Tabitha smiled and laughed. "And did I hear you say you had a meeting with Wes next week? I believe you'll need to return some rope to him from our date tomorrow. That's so sexy." She sighed.

Michael stared at her with a look of love. And lust. "That sigh. Anything you'd care to share, my hot wife?"

"I really liked you walking in to him fucking me the other night. Your face, even though you knew about it? Priceless."

"All of the blood in my body rushed to my dick in about three seconds. Don't even remember what I said. I'm sure there was cussing in it. You are so deliciously beautiful.

And that you like what I like so much, need it as much as I do? Luckiest man ever."

"It was hot and dirty to have you walk in on him fucking me. In our bed, but…"

"But what? You know you can tell me anything."

"I know." She averted her eyes because she knew she was keeping some things from him. Some feelings. It took her a second to look at him again. She didn't want to ruin their night by talking about anything negative, but there was something she really did want to talk to him about. "The dirtiness of fucking Wes in our bed and having you walk in was delicious, but it left me feeling a bit off."

"What do you mean by off?" Michael took another bite of corn and acted as if anything she said was going to be no big thing. That helped her keep going.

"I know he's been in the house a few times. Fucked me there, and it's always been fun and easy. Even in our bed. But the other night it almost felt like a violation to us. I liked the concept of it more than the actual act."

"Then we change the rules." He bobbed his eyebrows at her, which made her laugh. "Our extracurricular activities are just that. Pure fun and frivolity and dirty sex. If you have any misgivings about something, then we change them."

"Just like that? So, if I wanted to change the date this weekend to a hotel?"

"Of course. Absolutely change it. You having any reservations about a date is a red for me. And that goes for any of it. All of it."

"Awesome. Then I think that's exactly what I'm going to do." She may have just wanted to hear him say it. Confirm they were on the same page. The hotel was closer to his office by about ten minutes, which did it for her, too. She kept the last part to herself because she didn't want him to think she doubted him. Not for a second. Though him not making it for some reason had eaten into her thoughts several times.

Him missing their dinner the other night had left her even more shaken than she wanted to admit.

"Epic Friday dinner," he praised as he pushed his plate away a few inches. "With the best company a man could ask for. And the sexiest."

Tabitha wiped her mouth and leaned back in her chair as a gentle breeze ruffled her hair. "So good. I didn't realize I was that hungry." Staring at her husband, she sighed.

He reached for her hand, "Yes, my beautiful wife? Happy?"

"The happiest. Ever. As in...*ever*, ever. I needed this more than I think I knew." She shook her head and leaned toward him. "You. I needed you."

Michael's warm palm cupped her cheek. "Ditto. I know I've been working a lot, but it's all paying off. I honestly never thought the company could be this successful."

"It's not successful. You are. You make it successful because you work so hard. You're dedicated, which is one of the many reasons I fell in love with you so many years ago."

"And what are some of the other reasons?"

"You have a big cock and you do this thing with your tongue that makes my panties wet just to think about."

Laughter burst out of him and a few birds flew away from a tree at the back of the yard. "I love your honesty."

A bit of unease crawled up her spine and she shoved it back down. "So, how about we clean up and then veg in front of the TV? I also need to text Robin and make sure she sort of knows what she's in for."

"Sort of?" he asked as he pushed his chair back from the table.

She joined him and grabbed their plates to carry them back inside. "The hard part will be getting her up and ready by seventy-thirty. That girl is not a morning person. Then I'll let Logan bring the awesome when she's actually there."

Michael followed her inside with their wine glasses and the rest of what had been the table. "Good luck with that.

Go ahead and text her. I'll get things cleaned up and put up and go make sure the grill is taken care of."

"Great." Tabitha scraped the plates into the trash and set them in the sink.

As she turned, Michael trapped her between his body and the counter. "Have to pay the toll to pass." He wrapped his arms around her and she smoothed her palms up his biceps and around to his back.

"Oh, I do, do I? What would this toll consist of?"

He stared at the ceiling for a second before dropping his gaze to her again. "Two kisses. One now and one later."

"Later? What exactly is that kiss going to entail?"

One of his eyebrows lifted. "Oh, I'll make sure you don't miss the specifics of it when I request payment." Then his lips were on her. Her lips, jaw, throat. And he was all over her, loving her, seducing her.

She jerked against him as if she was about to come and wanted to beg as he rubbed his hardening cock against her pelvis. Just that fast she could go from a little horny to completely desperate for him.

As he pulled away it took her a second to get her eyes open. "Is the other kiss going to be anything like that?"

"Oh, yeah. But wetter. And on another set of lips." He kept going toward the back door.

"What? I thought I was going to be kissing you on another certain appendage."

"Only if you're a very good girl. I have a very big need to lick your pussy until you scream and then I'm going to make love to you till you come again. Or maybe fuck you until you scream again. I'm a little iffy on the specifics. Some things just need to be decided in the moment, you see."

"I see," she whispered to his back as he walked outside. She shook her head and put her cool hands on her cheeks. "Hottest. Man. And he's mine." With a shake of her head to try to clear it, she grabbed her phone from the counter and shot a text off to Robin. It took her several tries to get all the misspellings out of it. Autocorrect had a field day with her fuzzy brain.

Hey, neighbor. We're a go for tomorrow morning. Need you up and ready at 7:30 in the am.

Before she could put her phone down it dinged that she had a text back.

WTF.
You must have the wrong number.
Who is this?
Couldn't be Tabitha down the street because she knows I'm not functional until after 9.
Or 10.

You'll be just fine. I'll even buy you coffee on the way to cooking class. Oh, and bring an apron.

Oh, hell, no.
You want me up at 7:30?
In the morning?
And then you want me to cook?
Do you have a death wish?

"How's it going?" Michael asked as he stepped inside and locked the back door.

"It's taking some convincing. Hey, come take a picture for me." She turned the camera on and handed her phone to him. Clasping her hands together beneath her chin, she made an imploring face.

He snapped the picture with a chuckle and handed the camera back. "Having to pull out the big guns, I see."

"She's just playing hard to get."

His lips on her neck as he moved around her to the sink made her shiver and she had to try even harder to concentrate. Attaching the picture, she added, *Come on. It'll be fun.*

Ugh.
The pretty please face.

Is that a yes? ☺

Meh.
Fine.
7:30.
Do I need to pay for the class?
Other than with the life force you'll obviously be sucking out of me?

Ha!
Nope. The life force will be payment enough.
This will change your life. You'll see.

Uh-huh. Sure, it will. That coffee better be HUGE when you get here.

We'll go once I pick you up so you can get whatever size you like.

Deal.
Now I'm going to bed.
7:30. In the morning.
I must really love you.
SMH.
Night.

Night!

Tabitha added a ton of heart and kissing emojis to seal the deal before she put her phone back on the counter.

"I take that slightly evil *mwahaha* you just spouted was proof she said yes."

"You are correct. She'll be half-asleep until her caffeine kicks in, then she'll be ready to rock and roll."

Michael loaded the rest of the dishes in the dishwasher

and dried his hands. "I think you're just a few percent sadist."

"Me?" she asked with mock offense.

"You, my darling wife. Okay." He grabbed her hand and went toward the living room. "What do you want to watch? TV, movie, something recorded?"

"Not a movie. I'm already getting tired and don't want to fall asleep in the middle and not know how something ended. Ooh, can we watch that tiny house show I recorded? Those fascinate me. I could never do it, but…it's so fascinating."

"Perfect."

They collapsed on the couch and she grabbed the remote control. Less than a minute later the show she'd recorded earlier in the week was playing on the TV.

Michael got up.

"You okay?" she asked.

"Yep. Just gonna kill the lights." He flipped off the switches for the living room and cast the space into darkness, but for the light from the television.

Tabitha glanced outside. "Got dark." She glanced at the clock. "Nine-thirty? Really? I wondered why Robin was talking about going to bed."

Michael pulled his shirt over his head and tossed it at the floor by the end of the couch. His shorts followed. Then he pulled Tabitha to her feet and flicked open her shorts.

Fuck, she loved it when he handled her.

He stripped off her shorts and pushed her panties off with them. "Panties? Naughty, naughty." He tsked as he helped her step out of her clothes.

Elation filled her as she tugged her tank top over her head. "In my defense, you said you were going to be late."

"Mmm. Sans bra. No wonder I could see your nipples get hard earlier. I'll consider it an even trade. Such a good girl." He climbed onto the couch with his head on a pillow and his body along the full back of it.

Tabitha stretched out in front of him and snuggled into

his chest.

His warmth enveloped her immediately and he grabbed a thin blanket from the back of the couch to cover them with.

"I love you," she whispered in the near dark as he pulled her closer.

"Love you. So much." He kissed her hair and they settled against each other to watch the show.

A couple minutes later, she speculated how long he was going to be able to stay awake. He'd had another early morning and now they were full and they'd had wine and —

Michael's cock jumped against the flesh of her backside.

She froze, wondering if he was going to do something about it.

Then he settled against her and kissed her shoulder.

Another couple of minutes went by and his cock twitched once more. No more than a minute and it happened again.

The purr came from somewhere deep inside and she tilted her hips against him.

"Fuck. You so do it for me."

She lifted up a couple of inches to put herself at the right angle for him to take her, but he moved the other way, toward the opposite end of the couch.

"What are you doing?"

"There is a certain matter of a kiss that someone owes me."

"Oh."

He maneuvered her, rolling her onto her back, and settled between her thighs.

"I love it when you put me where you want me."

"Good. 'Cause I love putting you where you belong. Beneath me."

"Uhhhhh," she breathed out as he used the tip of his tongue to trace the outer edges of her pussy.

"So sensitive. So tasty." He flattened his tongue and licked her straight up the middle.

"You're not playing around tonight."

"I'm hungry, Tabby. Hungry for you."

"Ditto," she mumbled as he licked her again.

After pushing his hands beneath her thighs, he wrapped his arms around her until he could place his palms flat against her stomach. "You're already shaking. Do you like paying your toll, my pretty wife?"

"Love. It," she panted. She palmed her breasts and pinched her nipples.

"Need a little bit of an edge tonight?"

"I need exactly what you're doing. Huh," she huffed out as he moved lower and tongued her ass. He pushed the tip of his tongue through her tight muscles, throwing her even closer to coming on his mouth.

"I completely agree."

Tabitha nibbled her lip then spoke up, "Can I ask for something? A small something?"

"Of course." He licked her again and she almost forgot.

"Teeth marks. I'd like a few, please. Would love to have some reminders for a few hours when I sit down."

He kissed across to the inside of her thigh and gave her a bit of a nibble.

"Or a couple days." The whispered words turned into a gasp as he bit her. Hard.

Her entire body jittered as adrenaline flooded her bloodstream.

Squeezing her hands together, she tried to process the pain.

Letting go of the skin he'd marked, he licked the tender flesh. More pain traveled along her nerve endings to her head.

Another gasp echoed around them as he bit the other thigh.

Her clit pulsed and she almost came as he released her sensitive skin. "Best toll, ever," she declared.

He chuckled and licked upward. "Let this be a lesson to you." Reaching around with one hand, he pulled at the top of her sex, exposing her clit to the cool air and his warm mouth. "I thought about this all day at work."

"You did?" she asked as she pinched her nipples again. Trying to come or not to come, she really didn't know.

"All day. This right here. You pliant beneath me, taking the pleasure I want to give to you. Loving it. All. Day." He punctuated the last two words with the wet slide of his tongue around her clit. "Needing *us* as much as I do. The connection."

Pleasure raced through her and she had no doubt he was about to make her come. But she wanted something more. She wanted more of him. "Michael?" Her voice shook as she spoke his name.

"Yes, beautiful?"

"I'm gonna come. Soon."

"That's the plan."

"Can I make another request?"

He sucked her clit into his mouth and worked it with his tongue, giving her a gentle nibble. With one more gentle lick, he spoke against her mound. "Of course."

She had to swallow to get the words out. Not from embarrassment, but because she was that close to coming. "I really want to come with your cock in my mouth."

His mouth stopped moving and he shook his head. "I can't believe I didn't just blow my load all over the couch. Do you have any idea how you lay me low when you say things like that?"

"I need it. And thought that might be a little added bonus to the toll paying."

"Are you trying to bribe an officer of the law? You dirty girl." He bent to her pussy again and sucked on her clit.

"You're not actually an officer. Oh, fuck. Your mouth."

"Sure, I am. I got my degree at one of those online universities."

She arched against his mouth and tried to remember how to speak. "Umm, you can't actually do that online."

"Are you besmirching my double doctorate in criminal psychology and police...ness I got last week?"

"Yes." She laughed, which turned into a gasp, and her

entire body jerked. "You just bit me again."

"Yes, I did. I see how you're going to be. Only one thing I can do with that mouth of yours. Fill it."

He moved off the couch and his erection stood straight up. The tip glistened in the light from the forgotten television.

She tried to follow him but he pushed her shoulders back down. "Nope. I'll put you where I want you." Grabbing her hips, he pulled her down farther on the couch.

"Oh, God," she breathed out as he lifted her hips and turned her so her ass was planted on the back of the couch with her head hanging off the front of it.

The head of his cock, he pressed it between her lips and she got to suck the pre-cum from the end.

"Fuck," he cursed as he pressed in deeper. "Just. Fuck."

With her eyes closed and his balls pressing against her face, she wrapped her hands around his thighs and purred against his cock.

He split her legs wide and kissed the top of her mound.

The gentle kiss stopped her brain and switched it to some other kind of frequency. One where everything else in the world disappeared and all that remained was them.

"So wet, baby." His fingers rubbed her slickness around the entrance of her pussy then pushed inside. First one, then two. He massaged her G-spot as he tongued her clit. "Fuck, I love your fingernails in my thighs."

"Mmmmm," she hummed against his shaft. She hadn't even known she'd dug her nails into his legs. Her orgasm swirled inside her pelvis as she sucked his cock again and again with a bob of her head.

His knees against her shoulders and the edge of the couch kept her in place so he could reach down and pinch her nipples.

Threads of pleasure exploded from each place he touched her, claimed her.

She groaned and sucked him all the way into her mouth as delicious sensations raced outward to the top of her head and the tips of her curled toes.

"Come for me, Tabby. Come as you swallow my cock."

Her pussy and mouth pulled him in as she came. Whimpering on each contraction of her pussy, she bucked her hips as he tortured her clit.

The muscles in her pelvis twitched every few seconds and she panted as he pulled free from her mouth and her core.

"Stars. I see stars. Coming for you…" She didn't finish the thought. Him making her come always left her dazed and delirious with pleasure.

He shifted her until she lay sideways on the couch. "You coming for me. Fuck. It's mind-blowing."

As he stepped over to one of the end tables flanking the couch, she rolled to her knees on the floor.

"What do you think you're doing?" he asked as he opened one of the drawers in the table.

She flopped her upper body with her arms beneath her. Spreading her legs, she exhaled another moan. "Getting ready for my husband to fuck me, I hope."

"Half on the floor, half on the couch?"

"Mm-hmm. You can be behind me and grab on to the back if you need more…leverage."

"Oh, fuck."

"That is the plan." She laughed as he pulled lube from the drawer. "And when did you get all sneaky and put that down here?"

He popped the top and moved behind her. "This morning before I left for work."

The semi-coldness of the lube to her asshole was a delicious shock to her system. "This morning? I do love a man who has plans and makes them happen. I love a man even more who takes what he wants. So delicious."

The moment he pushed his cock into her sex, Tabitha groaned. She opened her mouth to speak but nothing came out. There was nothing she could say to tell him how perfect he made her feel in that moment.

Wanted.

Desired.

Loved.

Cherished.

All those things and more.

Then his thumb was in her ass. Two strokes then he switched to a finger. Then two. He spread the lube inside her, preparing her, enticing her.

"Your ass is so smooth. Tight. I love fucking it. Love taking it, because it's mine." He slid out of her pussy and fit his cock to her ass. With his palm on the base of her back, he urged her down a little farther. She spread her legs and relaxed as he pushed in.

Her arm shot out so she could grip one of the couch cushions as he popped past the ring of muscles he told her he loved stretching so much.

"Fuck…" they cursed together.

He grasped her hips. Pulling out, he paused for just a second then pushed back inside, one long thrust until his balls pressed against her clit.

Pleasure raced up her spine and she jerked and squeezed the cushion. "Fuck," she cursed again and her ass tightened around him.

He hissed behind her.

"I could come again," she told him with nothing short of a little bit of awe.

"Get your fingers on your clit. In your pussy. On your tits. Do what it takes to come. I want to fill you after you come on my cock. I need it, and it's not gonna be long before your ass sucks the cum from my balls. So. Fucking. Tight."

She circled her clit with the fingers on one hand. She didn't even remember moving her hands. She tugged up the mound of her sex with her other hand, doubling the sensation of delicious indulgence of him fucking her ass.

She squeezed her eyes shut and clamped her teeth together.

"Just like that. Fuck. I want it, Tabby."

She slipped her fingers in the juice sliding from her pussy and gathered some of it. She brushed against Michael's balls just because she could.

"Tabby," he growled. "Fuck."

She lightly scratched his sensitive sac with her nails and rubbed her clit in staccato little lines. Three passes. Four. That was all she needed as he filled her ass with his hard shaft. Wrapping her feet over Michael's calves, she anchored herself to him as she came.

Body. Mind. Soul. All connected.

Her orgasm pulsed through her groin in short bursts and Michael must have known. He fucked her ass with purpose, digging his fingers into her hips as he pumped inside her.

"Huh, huh," she exhaled and she thrashed beneath him, nearly shaking apart from the carnality of coming on his cock inside her.

So raw. Perfect.

Michael reached beneath her and grabbed her wrists, then twisted her arms until he had them pinned to the back of the couch. Leaning more of his weight against her, he trapped her beneath him.

She couldn't get away. Couldn't move.

"Take my cock, Tabby. Take it."

She screamed as he fucked her ass.

Pushing through her still spasming muscles, he shoved in as deep as he could get then…paused. "Tabby." Her name was an oath, a prayer. Something magical she'd need till the day she died. "My Tabby."

Tilting her hips as much as she could, she tried to get closer and begged for his cum. "Please, please give me your cum. I need it. Fuck, fuuucckkkkk," she screamed again.

He clamped down on her hands and eased her legs farther apart to get in deeper.

His weight on her kept her from floating away as he pumped his seed inside her.

"Tabby," he said again as pulse after pulse of cum shot into her ass.

The brush of his balls against her clit kicked off another mini orgasm and they both groaned as her ass locked down on him again.

He pulled out a couple of inches then pushed back inside and shivered against her flesh as he relaxed against her.

Too soon his weight was gone, but he stayed inside her as he coaxed her to the rug beneath their feet. They collapsed onto their sides, panting, trying to catch their breaths as the world slowly took shape around them again.

"I love you." His whispered words beside her came a second before he hugged her to him one more time.

Her purr for him was as natural as breathing and all she could offer, along with her smile of complete and utter satisfaction.

No other words were spoken. None were needed.

They lay there for a while. Together. Basking in the amazing afterglow of the best sex of her life.

Tabitha nodded off at one point, and came to when Michael had softened enough to slip from her ass.

"Let's go to bed, beautiful. I don't want you getting cold."

"Love how you take care of me."

"Always."

He carried her to bed as if she was some kind of princess in a castle and he was her prince who had come to rescue her. That was much more accurate than she would have ever thought possible. He was her prince. He was her everything.

She thought about talking to him as he tucked her into bed. The words were there to tell him what she'd been missing lately and how much she needed him and the life and connection they'd built together.

But maybe this was it. Maybe this was the path of everything getting back on track with them being together more.

Why would she bring up anything bad after the perfect evening they'd shared?

His voice whispered up her spine as he headed to his side of the bed. "You need anything before we crash?" He climbed in with her and she wouldn't have moved away from him for anything in that moment.

Holding his face, she kissed him as he pulled her close. "Just you, my husband. Just you."

Chapter Seven

Tabitha

A few minutes before eight o'clock on Saturday morning, Tabitha pulled on her apron in front of the table she and Robin were going to cook at. Her apron said 'Hot Stuff' across the chest. She glanced at Robin again and smiled. "That is the largest cup of coffee I've seen any coffee shop offer."

"Coffee. Mmm…" Robin took another drink and yawned hugely.

"What size is that? Fifty-five-gallon drum?"

Robin seemed as if she was trying to pry her eyelids apart and sort of looked around.

Tabitha's phone pinged a text and she pulled it out of her pocket and opened the screen. It was from Roland. She read it super quick, tried to hide her smile, shot an answer back and pocketed the phone again. Helping with a surprise for Robin totally delighted her.

The phrase 'sleeping while standing' came to Tabitha's mind when she glanced at Robin again. Tabitha laughed and Robin seemed to try to focus on her.

"I curse your bloodline for getting me out of bed this early."

Robin threw something else at her about pestilence and the plague but Tabitha couldn't follow it all behind her kissing the coffee cup.

"Better?"

"Mmm," she answered again and took another big swallow.

"Is that not burning your mouth? Seriously, that has to be so toasty still."

"Can't talk now. Caffeinating."

"A Homer Simpson reference? Really? And you said you weren't a morning person."

"This is not the morning. Morning has the good sense to not even start until after nine. This time of day is something else obscene all together. People don't call it the ass crack of dawn for nothing."

Tabitha laughed and drew a few stares from the other people in the class. They were all older. As in much older. She and Michael normally stood out. *Nothing new.* "And who are these *people* you're referencing?"

"People. I could tell you but then I'd have to kill you."

Glancing at the clock, Tabitha figured the chef was about to walk in. "Okay, you need your apron on. Coffee down. Apron on. You can do it."

Robin seemed a little bit more awake as she peered down for her apron.

"It's over your shoulder," Tabitha offered helpfully and laughed.

It seemed to take Robin some mental convincing to put her cup down, but she finally did part with it. "Hey. Naysayer. You'd better be glad I at least have clothes on. This early it wasn't guaranteed."

"Well, I appreciate you getting it done." Tabitha grabbed her chai latte and took a drink. Then promptly choked on it when she took in Robin's apron.

It wasn't just any apron she'd tied around her waist. *Oh, no.* It looked just like a half-naked beer fest girl. Little skirt, suspenders that barely hid the nipples and huge boobs were pictured front and center. The tops of stockings were the last thing before the apron cut off. And the girl on the apron could have been a dead ringer for Robin. That girl was stacked and then some. Tabitha had seen her naked a couple times, so she knew.

Yes, alcohol had been involved in those adventures, too.

Tabitha continued to choke and sputter on her coffee, which drew the attention of everyone in the kitchen. As if anyone could keep their eyes off Robin, anyway.

"You okay?" Robin asked with another yawn.

"Guess I should have been more specific on the kind of crowd we normally have here."

Robin glanced around. "What? Old people?" She muttered behind her cup with a smile as she took another drink.

"Umm." Tabitha grinned, already anticipating Logan's reaction to Robin. She rolled out of bed and resembled a supermodel. "Maybe."

"Mmm… Coffee."

"You are such a cheap date."

"Low-maintenance is my middle name."

"I thought your middle name was Bernadette."

"One of those." One more drink for her. It felt as if her cup was getting light. "Okay, tell me again why you dragged me out of bed at half past seven in the morning on a Saturday? There should be some kind of law against that."

"I'd already run a couple miles and showered before I came to get you. I could have come over way earlier."

"You would have been dead to me."

"Duly noted." Tabitha clearing her throat then took another drink and tried to keep her eyes off Robin's fake… ish nipples. "This class is really for basic cooking with a little bit of extra awesome. It's meatloaf and spaghetti and—"

"Linguini with scallops?" Robin asked with a fair amount of drooling.

"Exactly. Chef Logan gives one-on-one instruction while we cook and he tailors the menu based on requests from the class at the beginning of the course. His claim is that he can teach anyone to cook."

"Not likely. How long is the course?"

"Two months. Every Saturday."

Robin shook her head and nursed the last of her coffee with a quiet slurping sound. "At eight in the morning? You people seriously have to be masochists to do this for two months."

"May I remind you, you're here this morning."

"Under duress. No, no, no. I have a better one. I was *coerced*."

"With what?"

"Coffee. And I just want to be sure the quality of my cooking slave is up to par. See? Better. The coffee is working. I literally feel my snark meter rising. This is good. Okay. I'm here to give my slave a check-up. My final answer."

"You're a nut."

"Which is why we're such good friends. Nuts and berries go together."

"Berries?" Tabitha asked.

"'Cause you're so berry awesome!"

Tabitha chuckled. "You're definitely a nut."

"Honey roasted," Robin answered while peering around the kitchen.

"What are you looking for?"

"The chef who supposedly saves orphans on his downtime and farts rainbows and glitter."

"Orphans? Glitter?" Tabitha asked.

"Mm-hmm. Sounds like he might walk on water, too. What does he look like, anyway? Grandfatherly, big belly?"

The door to the kitchen opened and in walked Logan, wearing a crisp white chef jacket.

Robin's jaw hit the floor and Tabitha smiled. "Not exactly grandfatherly."

"Holy. Fuck," Robin whispered as Logan greeted a couple of people and headed to the front of the class.

Blond hair slicked back highlighted his surfer guy-worthy tan and ocean blue eyes that Tabitha was quite sure made many a pair of panties wet. He resembled most of Robin's hot wife dates. She hadn't realized it until Robin's tongue dangled about a foot out of her mouth.

Her attention was quite glued to Logan and Tabitha tried not to laugh.

"Good morning, everybody. Sorry I was a few minutes

late. Had to rescue a dog on the highway."

"See," Robin whispered and Logan glanced toward them then continued on with what the class was going to be about.

"Shh," Tabitha hushed her.

"Is he always in that coat?"

"Yes," Tabitha whispered and shushed her again.

"Hot. It's so white I think I need to put my sunglasses on. Ever seen him out of it?"

"No."

Logan glanced at them once more and smiled at Tabitha, then went back to pointing at something on the sideboard.

"If he got something on it I wonder if he'd take it off, 'cause, damn, I want to see what's under that coat."

"*Hmmhmm.*" Logan cleared his throat. "Is there something you'd like to share with the rest of the class?" He asked it staring right at Robin, and Tabitha half wanted to answer for her.

"Do you have a defibrillator in the classroom?"

"Uhh...no," he answered, probably trying to figure out what her question had to do with the class.

Tabitha sure wondered. Until Robin answered.

"Then nothing to share. Pretty sure the hearts in here wouldn't survive it." Robin smiled. *Talk about a knockout when she turned on the charm.*

Logan chuckled and turned back to the board.

Robin faced her and opened her mouth but Tabitha cut her off. "Nothing else until he's done talking. No...thing."

"Such a good girl," Robin whispered, but then she finally settled down.

Logan told them about what they were going to make in class. "Spaghetti and meatballs is on the menu for today, and a side dish suggested by Mrs. Angelica during the last course."

"What's the side dish?" someone asked from the other side of the room.

"Roasted rutabaga."

Tabitha burst out laughing and covered her mouth.

Lots of people turned toward her and she stared at the table to avoid them all.

Robin leaned over. "What's funny?"

"That's my safe word."

Robin snickered and tried to laugh silently. Her shoulders shook, which made Tabitha laugh again. "Epic," she mouthed.

Thankfully, they made it through the rest of the instruction without incident.

On the way up to the front of the class to gather their ingredients, Robin brushed Tabitha's backside and she gasped.

Robin jerked her hand away. "Dude. Sorry. Didn't mean to scare you that bad."

Tabitha glanced around, embarrassed, then smiled. "I'm just a little tender at the moment."

Robin's white teeth made an appearance. "Do tell," she prompted as they walked back to their table.

"Bite marks. Amazing. Totally what I needed to find some equilibrium again."

"You're so dirty."

"Hello, kettle."

"I completely agree. But I am so jealous. Have I told you how horny I am?" she asked as she stretched her neck and back. "Because I am. A lot."

"I do remember something about that."

Tabitha arranged their haul as Robin surveyed everything. Her horny cooking partner picked up a rutabaga then set it back down as if it might explode. "So, do we each make everything, or each of us takes a dish, or do we mud wrestle for it?"

"We work together."

"Thank the lord," Robin praised. "Or whatever I made was just going to have to be tossed. Food and I only get along one way."

"Which is?" A male voice asked the question and they

both looked up as Logan approached their table. "I'm Logan." He offered his hand along with a congenial smile.

"Robin." She shook his hand and Tabitha was pretty sure she shivered when she let go. "I eat it. That's it," Robin answered. "I can't cook. At all. Ask Tabitha. I can burn salad."

Logan raised an eyebrow and glanced at Tabitha.

"Yeah. That one is true. She put it in the oven. It wasn't pretty."

"In my defense…I truly can't cook."

"Wow. I've actually never heard of someone burning salad. That's impressive."

Robin rolled her eyes and tried to open a package of hamburger meat. She cut through the cellophane, the meat, the Styrofoam, and somehow got her knife stuck in the cutting board. "Not really that impressive." She shook her head. "I've done way worse. So, your claim that you can teach anyone to cook… Not actually feasible for some of us."

"Sure it is."

"Oh, ye of little faith at my ineptitude when it comes to cooking. Are you married?" Robin blurted out.

Tabitha didn't even try to hide her smile. She knew Robin was just making small talk to get to the kinky questions she really wanted answers to.

He held up his left hand. "Happily for nine years."

"And another one bites the dust," Robin sighed with a shake of her head.

Loud and snarky, she most definitely was. One thing she wasn't was a homewrecker. Tabitha was certain that was one of her and Roland's *rules*.

Robin yanked the knife out of the board and clipped the edge of their salt shaker on the way out. It fell over. Onto the meat.

Tabitha snickered as Logan righted the salt. He picked up the package of meat and stared at it. "That's quite a first, too. I do so like a challenge." He glanced at Robin's apron and cracked a smile as he walked away. "Nice apron."

"Just keepin' it real," was Robin's answer.

When he was far enough away she whispered to Tabitha, "Talk about pretty to look at."

"Yes, he is."

"Why didn't you tell me he was that yummy?"

"Hotness shouldn't matter when he's a great cook, and you need all the help you can get."

Robin pointed to her chest and added a fake pouty lip. "That hurts right here."

Tabitha smiled. "And I knew he was married, so it didn't matter. Plus, would it have helped the seven-thirty pick up? If I'd have known that I would have made you a pamphlet with his picture on it."

"Oh, hell, no. Nothing can make up for that." She glanced up, to where Logan had been. "So, did we lose our meat? Are we only going to make your safe word side dish now?"

Tabitha closed her eyes. "Oh, my God, I was so not ready for that side dish."

"Here you go, ladies." Logan walked up with a new package of meat, or it could have been their old meat washed off. It was already open and on a plate. And he handed it to Tabitha.

"Don't trust me with your meat?" Robin asked with a smirk.

"I don't even trust you with tossing my salad now," he joked right back.

"Good call," Tabitha agreed with a laugh.

"And I have something special for you to use during class while you're cutting up veggies."

"What is it? I hope you invented something equivalent to the bumper guards when you bowl, 'cause that's probably the only thing that's going to help me."

"Something like that." He reached into his pocket and pulled out a glove. A metal glove. Made out of chain mail. "Which hand do you hold the knife with?"

"My right," Robin answered. "Sort of."

"Hold out your left hand then."

She did and he slipped the glove over her hand.

"This is so you don't cut your fingers when you're cubing the rutabaga." He clicked a latch around her wrist to hold it in place.

"This is awesome. I feel like Michael Jackson." She waved her hand around and turned in a circle. "Does this really work?"

"We'll know by the end of class if you still have all of your digits."

"Haven't you tried it out before?"

"Never had anyone I thought warranted its special qualities."

"Aww. That's the nicest way anyone has insulted my cooking."

"Just keepin' it real," he fired back with another gorgeous smile.

"You little thief, you stole my line."

He shrugged. "What can I say? In some cultures, copying is the ultimate form of flattery."

"And in some cultures, plagiarism is punishable by five to ten."

Logan chuckled. "Well played."

Robin bowed.

"I'm gonna go check around with everyone. Holler if you need me." He wandered to the next table.

"I wonder if anything ruffles him?" Robin asked as she stared at the cool glove again.

"He's supposedly a C.I.A. graduate. Owns a couple restaurants. Is super successful."

"How do you know all that?"

"Michael built the restaurants a year and a half ago."

"Very cool. Okay." She lowered her hand and jiggled the metal glove like a bangle bracelet. "Put me in, coach. I wanna chop stuff."

"Great attitude. I knew Logan could work some magic."

"Hey, I'm not that bad."

"Uhh. You put a Styrofoam container in the oven with the salad and burned both of them."

"Oh. Right. Yowza. That was a bad dinner."

Tabitha laughed and grabbed the rutabaga. "How about I'll peel and then you can cut with your robo hand protection?"

"Deal."

A few minutes later, Robin was cubing the rutabaga like a champ and was actually quiet while she concentrated on not hitting the metal. Much better catching the glove than her hand but Tabitha loved her focus. It was incredibly cute to watch.

Tabitha mixed up the seasonings in the hamburger meat and added the rest of the ingredients for the meatballs. While she made them into balls, she wanted to talk. "Guess what?"

"What?" Robin asked.

"Michael came home early last night. And surprised me."

"No shit. He left work early. Really?"

"And we had a date. Ate outside, grilled and had wine and other stuff."

"Oooooo." Robin added a teasing whistle at the end. "What kind of stuff? Other than teeth marks? Lucky girl."

"The best kind," she whispered as she finished rolling the meat and switched to chopping tomatoes and mushrooms for the sauce.

"And did you have a chance to talk to him about... things?"

Tabitha wrinkled her nose. "I didn't want to ruin the night. Couldn't fathom messing up what could be the start of everything slipping back into place."

"Things slip out of place. People have to work to put them back together. Is that the only reason you didn't want to bring things up?"

"No. I just don't want to rock the boat. Nope. That's a lie. Actually, I just don't want to deal with it at all. I'd rather bury my head in the sand, thank you very much."

Robin nodded. "I get that, but there's a problem. It's gonna keep eating at you. I know it."

"How do you know that?"

"Because you're a girl and we let things get to us. It'll keep cropping up until you talk to him. And…"

"What?" She paused in her getting the sauce ready to cook so she could stare at her best friend for her sage advice.

"I just made that rutabaga my bitch."

Tabitha laughed, and so did a few other people around them.

"Did I hear you still have all your fingers?" Logan asked as he walked around from behind them.

"Totally." Robin waggled her fingers.

"Now all you need is a little bit of olive oil." He supervised her drizzling it on. "And some salt and pepper. Not as much as you put on the meat. A little less than that. Say a pinch or so will do."

"Party pooper." Sprinkling on the salt and pepper, Robin stared at the rutabaga and beamed. "I totally made that."

"And the pieces look great. Good size and all pretty uniform. You could be a prep chef in the making."

"Seriously."

"Absolutely. They prep all the food. They're wicked important."

"When do they have to arrive?"

"If there's a breakfast service normally five or five-thirty."

"In the morning?"

Logan smiled. "That is normally when breakfast is served."

"I wouldn't hold your breath then. This is probably the only time you'll see me this early in the morning. As in ever."

"You never know. Cooking can get in your blood."

"And so can staph. It's why they make antibiotics."

Logan shook his head and wandered away.

"You ready to cook it now?" Tabitha asked.

"Oh, lord. Me and the oven might actually be mortal

enemies."

"Nope. You'll be just fine. One for all and all for —"

"The fire extinguisher!"

* * * *

A couple hours later, Logan walked them out at the end of class in the dirtiest chef jacket Tabitha had ever seen him in.

"Hope you enjoyed the class," he told both of them.

"I sure did," Robin praised as she jiggled their to-go containers. "And, uhh, sorry about the jacket. That ladle just kind of got away from me."

"That's actually happened to me before. The second time it got away from you was a bit of a surprise, though." His eyes went wide and Tabitha wondered what he was really thinking.

Tabitha laughed and patted him on the back. "Thanks for being such a good instructor. I knew if anyone could help her it was you."

"I loved putting your motto to the test," Robin admitted. "It was actually fun. And thanks for letting me keep the glove. I promise to put it to good use."

"The next course starts in a few weeks. You should think about bringing your husband and joining."

"Hey, Logan," someone called behind them.

He glanced back for a second and faced them again with a mischievous grin. "Duty calls."

Then he was gone again to talk to someone else from the class.

As they pushed through the doors to outside, Tabitha asked, "What do you think? Would you come back?"

"I think I actually would. Even if I have to get up before it's legal in the state of North Carolina."

"That's not actually a thing."

"Oh, it sure will be when I bring it up to the next neighborhood association meeting. There will be petitions and signs. T-shirts, even." Robin's phone dinged in her purse. "Ooh, ooh, ooh, that's Roland. Can you hold the food for a second?"

"Of course."

"Hopefully he's on his way home. Hopefully by the time we get...there..."

"What is it?" Tabitha asked, already knowing what it was about.

"It says, 'nice apron'. But I didn't send him a picture of myself in it while we were in there. How does he know – ?"

"I believe the man you're looking for is right over..." Tabitha turned to the right, where Roland had texted her that morning that he'd be. "There." She pointed and Robin bounced up and down.

Her best friend took off across the parking lot. Thankfully, she checked both ways when she needed to. She leaped on her husband as soon as she was close enough.

Tabitha smiled and followed at a slower pace.

Robin's husband was a looker, just like her. With his red hair and green eyes, they made a striking couple. His parents were full-blooded Scottish, but no one could tell it when he spoke. Unless his nickname for Robin slipped out.

'Lass.'

Siiiigggghhhh.

Roland lowered Robin to the ground as Tabitha approached.

"Hey, Roland. Fancy meeting you here."

"You knew!" Robin accused and hugged her husband again.

"Guilty."

"I texted her this morning, lass, and told her I'd meet you here. Didn't want to wait for you to get home. I missed you too bad."

"Missed you so bad. Oh, my God, and I had to get up at seven o'clock and I cooked spaghetti and meatballs and rutabaga."

"I have the proof right here." Tabitha held up the

containers and handed them to Roland.

To his credit, he took them, but he did hold them a ways away from his body.

"No, no. It's actually edible. We'll have to make pasta for dinner tonight because I might have ruined ours. But the sauce and the side dish are totally edible. We tried them."

"And you didn't die yet?"

Robin opened her mouth and huffed out a breath at him. "Nope, but if I'm going down you're coming with me." She pulled his face closer to hers and kissed him soundly.

"They're actually both awesome and she did great," Tabitha offered as she dug for her keys. "I'm gonna get out of here. I have things to do at home to get ready for tonight."

"Don't do anything I wouldn't do," Robin told her.

"Well, that leaves a very open playing field."

"Exactly."

Tabitha leaned forward and kissed Robin's cheek, since she knew she wasn't going to separate from Roland willingly for the next few…days. "Thanks for coming with me, and think about what Logan said. I think you really would like the whole class. You, too, Roland." She stepped a few spaces back toward her car.

"I'll think about it. Have fun tonight."

"I will," she called over her shoulder and blew Robin a kiss.

It didn't take her long to get into her vehicle and pull out of her parking spot.

She laughed hysterically as she passed behind Roland's SUV, and she stopped to take a picture.

Roland's head could be seen through the back window.

Robin's? Nowhere to be found.

Tabitha took a picture and texted it to Michael with the caption of 'Roland's home'.

A string of laughing emojis came back.

Tabitha put her phone in the middle cup holder and pulled out into traffic.

She needed to get home and get finished packing for

tonight.

A hotel room and a whole lot of dirty business had her name on them, and she had every intention of enjoying it.

Chapter Eight

Tabitha

When she walked into the house, she checked her phone again.

Michael had texted that he'd gotten lots done already for the project he was working on for Wes.

One of his biggest clients.

And the man she was planning on meeting tonight in a hotel room to have wicked dirty sex with.

She set her stuff down and headed upstairs with her phone.

The idea of her being a perk of their business dealings did it for her in quite a few delicious ways.

When Michael had still been working for his former company Wes had been one of their biggest accounts. Michael had been assigned his file and they'd hit it off. Tabitha had stopped by to see Michael at work and to take him to lunch. Wes had been there going over some kind of plan. The attraction had bubbled under the surface and they'd ended up all going to lunch that day.

Before going back to work, Tabitha had ended up being fucked in the men's bathroom. Twice.

It hadn't been the first time she'd been a hot wife, but it was one of the most memorable firsts.

Her pussy clenched as she moved through her bedroom. She set her phone on the corner of the bed and headed to the closet. Grabbing things for her date with Wes that night made her pussy wet. Imagining Michael's reaction to her being tied up when he arrived… So dirty. Tying her in the rope Wes had made himself, he said he liked knowing he was the only one to touch the strands before binding her with the tight jute.

She shivered and actually swayed on her feet, knowing the look that would be in Michael's eyes when he opened the door to the hotel room. He loved her in rope. Sometimes Wes would leave her tied up so Michael could fuck her in it, too, before he untied her.

Then Michael would just take the rope back to him the next week. At work. So intense. Kinky.

Lucky. Blessed.

Whatever she was, she thanked the fates for putting her with a man as amazing as Michael. Knowing how much he loved her and everything he gave her was another reason she was finding it so hard to bring up the things bothering her.

She should just be able to get over it.

She wanted to.

It sure would make her stress level better, but she just couldn't get there.

Chewing on the inside of her lip, she snagged the pair of heels she wanted to take with her and put them in her suitcase.

The night before, with Michael having coming home early, had made her feel almost reset.

His excitement about his new clients had been palpable, and talking with him before, during and after dinner about what he had going on had delighted her.

He'd given her several openings to bring up some of her concerns and she just hadn't taken them. The words had stuck in her throat and her chest had gotten tight each time she'd tried.

The reasons for moving her date with Wes to a hotel were valid.

Mostly.

But she'd realized earlier that one of the other reasons she wanted to have the date at a hotel was so they could have a little distance. Her and Michael. Not from each other, but more into a neutral kind of space so they could talk afterward.

Really talk.

Coming clean with how she was struggling needed to happen. Being what she was to her husband didn't allow her the luxury of lying by omission. She was bound in more ways than one to be open and honest about everything. Even her fears and emotions, which she wanted to avoid at all costs. Those rules being followed were an absolute she'd been avoiding for weeks.

She took a deep breath and made a decision.

No more.

No more hiding.

No more waiting to talk to him.

Not when she respected their dynamic, not when she respected the man she submitted to. Kneeling for him, giving him her power, turned her on, but she couldn't pick and choose just the easy pieces anymore.

Part of moving the date was tied to not wanting anything negative to happen in their home. Their walls were sacred and she wanted to keep them that way. Especially if she was going to let him see her vulnerable—and she didn't mean physically.

The physical part was almost always easier.

After she played, her walls would be down more than at any other time. When Michael took care of her afterward, she knew that would be her most comfortable time to finally open up about the missed plans and lack of connection. She'd done a lot of thinking after she and Robin had spoken the other night and at the cooking class. Being chickenshit about her concerns wasn't going to get her anywhere, so she was going to suck it up and deal with the hard stuff.

That she still, after all the time since her ex, had to consciously make an effort not to emotionally run away from something pissed her off.

She'd take pissed off over panicked any day. Hiding the

panic, even from herself, had been a coping mechanism she'd employed for as long as she could remember.

"Andrew. Such a douche."

She nodded to her suitcase as if it could give her a fist bump and she headed to the bathroom to grab a few more things.

She'd packed some things that morning after she'd gone for her run, so it was just after noon and she had almost everything ready.

Except Michael.

Him going in for a few hours to get some preliminary things done on the Beaufort project had absolutely been her idea. And she still thought it was a great idea and helped both of them.

But…

Ugh.

What if he forgot again?

What if he forgot *her* again?

That was it.

Her.

Him forgetting a date or an event made her feel off. Him forgetting her when she needed him would be catastrophic.

She didn't want that to happen.

Not at any cost.

Glancing out of the bathroom, she eyed her phone sitting on the corner of the bed.

Tabitha was done playing games to see if he checked things like he used to.

Busy could be worked around and she wanted to make sure tonight happened with no more issues.

It didn't take her long to grab the stuff she needed out of the bathroom, pack it and snag her phone. She headed toward her favorite chair by the window. As she stared over the back of the chair, she could see the downtown skyline. It was almost like looking at her husband. His office was right by the one third from the left.

As she got situated in the chair, something white by the

wall, on the floor, caught her attention.

"What is that?"

Once up and out of the chair, she crouched down by the wall. A giggle bubbled out of her.

A white button.

Wes' white button.

"So delicious." She pocketed it and resettled in the chair with the window at her back.

After pulling up Michael's text screen, she hit the button to take a picture.

With a smile, she angled herself in the chair so the building above his was close to her face through the window. She held the camera out, acted as if she was licking the building and snapped the selfie.

Thinking of you, she captioned the photo before sending it.

It took only a few seconds for him to respond.

Fuck. That completely shut me down. Like…my brain can't function past the awesome to cum

Yeah! Totally the truth. Getting everything packed for tonight. Horny. Thought you needed to know.

Yes, I did.
You heading over early to shower and get ready?

Yep.

She glanced at the clock.

I'll probably leave in a couple hours. Might even take a nap before I go since I'm done packing all my girlie stuff. Want to make sure I'm well-rested to be used tonight.

Used. Double Fuck.
Literally.

You'll be there around 6:30 or 7, right? I'll be more than ready for you to be there by then if Wes shows up at 6. Then we can talk and have dirty sex and crash till tomorrow morning. It'll be like a mini vacation.

All good. I'll be there. Hard.

Hard, huh? How will I recognize you??

She tucked her feet beneath her and waited. Her phone beeped and a picture filled the screen. Michael's pants. Tented.

I'll make sure you get properly acquainted when I arrive.

Deal!

As if you had a choice.

Siiggghhhhh…

Okay. Clients are on the way.

Panic kicked up and she bit her lip.

Uhh…clients?

Going in for a few hours turned into a meeting with the Beaufort museum clients. They happened to be in the city and free when I called to ask them a few questions.
Since we couldn't find a time to meet the following week it seemed pretty perfect, so…

Deep breath in, deep breath out.
She started to type a question she hated to ask. *You won't forget our date, right?* But before she could send it Michael texted.

Don't worry.

I won't forget our date, baby.
And I have to get rid of my hard-on now. What you do to me.

She erased the text she'd almost sent and took another breath. Levity sounded better than scared so she went with flirty plus a little bit of snark.

You're welcome.

For what?

Your hard-on. ☺

Fuck, I love you.

Love you, my husband. Kick ass. See you in a few hours. On my knees.

Will!
Damn.
Down, boy, down!

Smiling, she got up and set an alarm on her phone for an hour and a half. A nap sounded great but she didn't want to oversleep. She flipped up through his texts to stare at the pic of his lap one more time before she set the phone on the nightstand.

Moving her suitcase to the side, she then climbed under the covers on Michael's side of the bed so she could smell his pillow.

She closed her eyes and snuggled in to sleep.

It definitely sounded as if she was going to need it.

Luckiest. Girl. Ever.

* * * *

Hours later, looking in the mirror at the hotel, Tabitha applied a thin layer of pink lip gloss, which was the final

115

piece of her makeup regime so she felt sexy and pretty. She rubbed her lips together and tossed the small tube of makeup back into her bag on the bathroom counter and zipped it up. Turning to the right and left in front of the full-length mirror, she made sure everything was perfect. Her hair was loose down her back and her skin was freshly lotioned after a quick shower.

She'd done this quite a few times in the past few years with different partners, as Michael and she had decided to make changes, and she'd never been as nervous as she was for this one.

Feeling uneasy about her and Michael wasn't something she was used to, so she felt lost on how to process the worry.

It didn't take a psychology degree to figure out she was scared about the talk afterward with Michael. He didn't even know she wanted to talk, and lying to him didn't sit well with her. Not at all. Lying by omission reeked of keeping secrets because she was purposefully keeping it to herself. She hated being anxious about how the conversation was going to go.

She'd never been so worried to talk to him. He was always understanding and allayed her fears. *So why does the thought of talking to him make me nauseous? And why am I worried he's going to be late?* Pushing away from the counter, Tabitha padded into the bedroom on bare feet. "I'm being silly. I'll just text him and make sure everything is fine."

As she headed toward the nightstand sitting between the two queen-sized beds, a text came through. Michael's text tone.

Is Wes there yet?

No. She glanced at the clock. Five-fifty-five.

Should be anytime now. Why?

Two seconds later the display lit up with a picture of her and Michael on their wedding day. The image she'd saved to his profile always made her happy when he called. She swiped the screen. "Hi," she kind of breathed into the phone.

"Fuck, Tabby. When you answer the phone in that voice it's a mystery how I have any blood north of the equator to continue with the phone call."

She smiled and sat on the edge of one of the beds. "Love rendering you speechless."

"Try brain-dead. Holy hell, you take over every thought in my head."

"Thanks," she added with a smile. "I'm glad you called."

"You are?" he asked, with a whole lot of 'tell me more' in his voice. "Missing me, my beautiful wife?"

She paused for a moment and closed her eyes. "A lot." Feeling silly for her earlier worry, she decided not to start anything over the phone. The conversation they had to have was definitely something that needed to happen in person. "Everything okay? I figured you'd be on the way out the door by now. You got the picture of the room number, right?"

"I got the pic. Best wife ever. I'll just be a little bit late. So, I wanted to call and tell you to start without me. I'll join the party as soon as the meeting is done."

"The meeting isn't over yet?" Her voice went a bit high at the end.

"No, baby. Just a little bit longer. We're almost done. I'll be there in a little while."

Her heart stuttered as if it was deflating like a popped balloon. "Do you promise?" Her voice. It didn't even sound like hers. It sounded — scared.

"I promise, baby. I won't let you down. Not once."

The anxiety flooding her system dissipated to a somewhat manageable level. Michael had never broken a promise to her. Not ever. If he said the words then he'd do anything to keep them. Realizing that helped her push the worry down a bit farther.

"Are you positive you don't want me to just cancel with

Wes? I'm sure he'd be more than understanding."

"No doubt he would. But you're already showered and dressed and horny, right?"

Her laugh slipped out and she took a deeper breath. "Correct on all three." Him knowing her so well helped her shove the panic into a drawer marked 'later'.

"Then it's fine. Enjoy yourself and remember all the juicy details. You can tell me all about it when I fuck your ass after I get there."

Her heart stuttered in her chest one more time, but this go-round it was for all the right reasons. "Deal. Love you, my husband."

"Love you, my wife. Always."

Knock, knock, knock. "I think Wes is here. See you in a little while?"

"Fuck, yes. Hottest wife on the planet. And you're mine. Luckiest man ever."

"Luckiest wife ever. Love you."

"Love you more than anything. And, Tabitha?"

She bit her lip and smiled. "Yes?"

"Can't wait for my sloppy seconds." And he was gone.

Need and love and hope and trust swirled inside her as she pushed the off button. She fumbled with the phone for a second, almost dropping it, then set it on the nightstand beside the bed in case Michael needed to reach her.

Glancing at herself in the mirror, she made sure her pink-and-black negligee still looked good. If her date was as on point as he normally was she wouldn't be wearing anything for very long. She slipped into her six-inch heels and closed the distance to the door. Anticipation bubbled inside her and she sought that warm, comfortable place she only found in submission.

It was like coming home, and she knew she was exactly where she was supposed to be. She bit her bottom lip, excited to talk to Michael later. She already couldn't wait for him to get there.

Subspace called to her and she listened to its whispered

comfort as it pulled her closer and closer to her happy place.

Peering through the peephole —

There he was. Wes. Sleek hair, piercing gray eyes. Staring right back at her as he adjusted a duffle bag hooked over his shoulder.

One nervous swallow and a deep breath later, she unlatched the chain and opened the door.

His gaze bored into hers and he just stared at her for a second. Head to toe, he seemed to take in everything. And she'd played with him enough to know it wasn't just a visual assessment he was doing. He always noticed her elevated breathing, the way she rolled her lips and bit them, her flushed skin, her goose bumps and her scent. He noticed all of it. He'd told her before each thing he observed made a picture of how she was, what she needed, what he would do to her.

Taking a step forward, he tossed his bag down. He crowded into her space, kicked the door closed then grabbed a handful of her hair. "You smell good." He pulled her head to the side and sniffed up her throat, then went back for a second pass, but this time he used his tongue. "Fuck. Taste good, too. You ready for me, Tabby Cat?"

"Y-y-yes, Sir." Just that fast, he turned her head off and it was all she could do to stay on her feet.

"I love it when you get nervous around me. Why is that, do you think? I mean, we've been playing together for what? Three years now."

Nothing else but honesty would work in that situation. "Because you scare me a little," she whispered.

He paused for a second, a slow grin pulling up his lips. "Good." After whipping her around, he shoved her face first toward the door and hiked up the bottom of her cute outfit. His growl kicked up another round of goose bumps as he tore her panties from her hips. Yanking at the closure of his slacks with one hand, he then lifted her leg with the other. The head of his cock nudged the entrance to her sex. "So fucking tight. Love having to work for it. This might hurt a little."

She opened her mouth to say something, but instead she cried out as he entered her with one long thrust.

He pulled out, grabbed behind her knee and lifted her leg even higher then pushed back inside. "Fuck. So wet, Tabby Cat. I think you need this almost as much as I do."

"More," she forced out through gritted teeth. She didn't want to beg. Not this early. He'd just drag it out longer because he'd know how much she wanted it.

He reached around her to roll the tips of his fingers across her clit.

"Uhhh," she whispered and closed her eyes.

"Feel good?"

His breath on her cheek made her bite her lip again. "Yes."

"You just got wetter, you dirty girl." He thrust until his balls touched the lips of her sex. His cock jerked once, again, then he pulled out.

A whimper slipped free.

He chuckled and lowered her leg. "I love the noises you make. Can't wait to hear them with my handprint on your ass."

The straps to her outfit slipped from her shoulders when Wes slid them off, then he shoved the sheer fabric down over her hips.

"So delicious. Clothing barely on. Beautiful. But nothing is better than you naked." He tossed the material on the bed and eyed her again. "Kick off the shoes, too. I have plans for you." Shoving at his pants, he then ditched those as she got rid of her shoes. Quickly they were both naked. "On the bed, Tabby Cat. Sit back on your heels with your back facing me. You and I have a date with a new batch of six-millimeter jute I just finished processing this morning."

"That's going to be scratchy." She walked over to the bed and climbed on, not at all displeased with the idea of longer-lasting rope marks.

"Such a lucky girl you are, to help me break it in."

"Thank you, Sir."

"You are so very welcome." Grabbing his bag, he then set it on the corner of the bed. He unzipped it and pulled out three or four bundles of natural fiber. The tied ends were his normal style. The rope was wound tight just like he always did, but it was obviously not coiled as it normally was. "It's gonna take me a few minutes to recoil this. I didn't want to be late so I wound it up and put it in." He glanced up at her. "Plus, I liked the idea of you watching me wrap it, knowing full well it was just to taunt you."

She shivered, knowing how delicious the rope would feel on her skin—abrasive yet still soft somehow as it moved across her flesh.

"I can smell your pussy juice. So dirty. Get your fingers on your clit. Little circles, soft, teasing. I want you dripping by the time I put your hands behind your back."

Tabitha slid her fingers onto her sex before he finished speaking. She already knew he wouldn't let her come. Not yet. Not until he tied her up. Bound her. Made her beg for it.

Over her shoulder she watched him.

Standing beside the bed, cock jutting from his hips, he taunted her just as much as the rope did. That man was potent. Second sexiest man she'd ever been with.

Her entire body shuddered as he finished the last rope, she spread the wetness sliding from her core.

"Let me see those fingers, dirty girl."

She held them up and jerked again as he sucked one then another into his mouth.

"Delicious." He licked the tip of one slick digit, staring at her.

Heat rose from her chest, working its way higher.

"You're the perfect mix of innocent and wicked, Tabby Cat."

"Thank you, Sir."

He reached back into his bag and brought out a blindfold.

Tabitha automatically swiveled back around to face the wall.

Wes slipping the material over her eyes made her heart race. It pumped hard, and the rest of her senses kicked into a higher gear to make up for the loss of her sight.

His hand caressing along her spine brought on a full moan. The low guttural sound shocked her and she cut it off, clamping her teeth together.

"I want to hear you. Don't stifle your reaction or I'll be forced to push a few of your buttons."

That thought both excited and terrified her.

After positioning her arms behind her, he wound the rope about her wrists. Once. Twice.

The rope against her skin already had her sinking into that magical place where bondage took her. Some ethereal location so high she couldn't see the ground anymore. Where she felt no fear and grew ever closer to the man who possessed every piece of her.

Michael.

Wes wrapped the rope around her chest twice and tied it in the back, creating a stem. He secured it under her arms and repeated the process beneath her breasts. Each pass bound her to him, pulling her tighter under his control. His dominance. He was careful of her hair as he tied her, making sure it didn't get caught in the rope. Such a simple gesture, but she focused on it, anticipating each shift of his body against hers as he finished her chest harness.

Being tied by Wes was amazing. Him fucking her while she was in his rope? Unbelievable.

"Open."

Something smooth brushed against her lips and she followed his instruction. A latex ball fit between her teeth, barely, and he fastened the gag behind her head.

"So sexy."

He bit her shoulder and her *unf* around the gag made him bite harder. Or so she thought as she squeaked through the pain.

"My teeth marks on you. Fuck. Michael's definitely going to see that one when he gets here." He brushed her hair to the other side then wrenched a handful of it until she yelped. "Pretty sure you need a matching set." After tilting her head to the side, he bit her again. Hard.

Her torso quivered and she wanted to rub her legs together, but she didn't. Because he hadn't told her to.

She sucked in a sharp breath as he yanked her up onto her knees by the hold he had in her hair. Pleasure raced to the top of her head and she squeezed her eyes shut when he pushed two fingers into her greedy sex.

"You realize you're going to have to earn my cock tonight, right? Especially after I made an extra trip to see you earlier this week."

"Uh-huh," was all she could manage around the gag.

He flipped her over across his lap and slapped her hard on one cheek, then the other. Back and forth, again and again. She lost count almost immediately.

His fingers slid through the juicy wetness between her thighs and he filled her pussy again. "So fucking soaked."

He found a rhythm set to erase any composure she had left, but too soon he pulled his fingers away. He squeezed one of her cheeks then swatted her again.

"My handprint. Here. Here. I can already see how pink your ass is going to be when I'm done with you." He traced the outline of a mark he'd put on her.

The soft touch was almost too much to take.

So devilish. The sensation of hard and soft pushed her buttons so aggressively and he knew it.

She couldn't process the needs running through her before he'd already switched to the other kind of touch. Both equally destroyed any barriers she tried to put up between them.

"There she is," Wes whispered.

Tucking her head against the side of the bed, she tried in vain to hide from him. But he knew her body so well that not being able to see her face changed nothing.

Her panting breaths expanded inside the room as he filled her pussy again.

"I feel you clamping down on my fingers, getting ready to orgasm." He pulled his hand away and she whined at the loss of sensation. "I know how close you are." Moving her again, he put her chest down on the bed but her lower half was still up on her knees so her ass was in the air. His five o'clock shadow brushed her thighs a moment before he lashed his tongue along the sensitive lips of her sex. "I wanted a taste before I fuck you."

The mattress dipped and she heard the foil of a condom package ripping right before he climbed on behind her. Then he was there, surging forward, pushing in deep. One. Long. Thrust.

His balls touched her clit and she was instantly ready to come. Her muscles clamped down on him and he clenched his jaw shut for a second. "Your pussy is like a Dyson, baby. You suck me in. The pleasure your body gives me…" His hand came crashing down on her upturned ass again.

She fisted her hands behind her back, over and over against the opposite arms she held on to because of the harness binding her upper limbs together.

As if he'd heard her thoughts, he grabbed onto the stem at her back.

"The perfect handle," he told her as he used it to fuck her even harder. Deeper.

She tightened her fists as he fucked her.

"Hurt?" he asked her as he pushed in farther.

Nodding with a grunt was all she could do with her jaw locked around the gag.

"Good."

He pushed her down on the bed, kneeing her thighs wide so he could take her. With one hand in her hair, he pushed the other between her and the mattress. "Wet pussy, Tabby Cat. I think somebody likes it rough."

Responding wasn't an option.

All she could do was ride his fingers as he rubbed her clit.

A keening cry erupted from inside her when she came.

"Fuck, yes. Just like that. Come for me," he commanded

in her ear. He bit her earlobe. "Give it to me. Such a dirty little hot wife, coming on my cock and fingers."

Her entire body thrashed beneath his and he put more weight on her, trapping her arms between them.

And his fingers never stopped moving. Never.

She came again with a wail, trying to shake her head, but she couldn't fight the hold he had on her hair.

"Your pussy gets so tight when you come. You're gonna suck the cum from my balls." He pulled out of her and off to the side of the bed. "Fuck. I'm gonna come all over your face. The gag. The blindfold." He reached back between her legs as she panted, trying to catch her breath. "Your wet pussy on my palm. So dirty."

He gathered her slick juices on his hand, and the scent of her pussy reached her nose as he came closer.

The rhythmic beat as he jacked his cock was all she could hear. Then his hand landed on her ass.

She jerked, twisting on the bed to get away from the pain — or find more.

"Fuuuccckkkk."

His cum landed across her lips and the gag. The second stripe of his possession hit her on the cheek. Her abdomen contracted as he came and he grabbed her ass, squeezing the marks he'd made.

"So. Dirty," he praised, and another pulse of cum hit her chest.

Her body relaxed, the pain and pleasure mixing together until she floated free of everything into a magic location called subspace. Nothing could touch her there. No worry or fear. Only happiness and pleasure.

The high from Wes spanking her, making her come, coming on her, was only eclipsed by one thing.

Getting to tell Michael about it while he was deep inside her ass.

She sighed and took a deep breath, wondering if he'd come in during the scene.

Time ceased to run normally during a scene with Wes.

Afterward was always a slideshow of certain moments she remembered, but things got lost in the middle.

She remembered groaning when he took the gag out and his chuckle that followed. Then the cool air from the room's A/C as he wiped off her face with a warm cloth.

The soreness of her arms settled in as he climbed back onto the bed and removed her harness.

Then he pulled off the blindfold. The lights were so bright as she struggled to see.

It took her a little bit to focus when she opened her eyes. Glancing around…

No Michael.

Dread grew inside her but she pushed it back. Maybe he'd gotten stuck in traffic.

"Let's get you under the covers so you don't get cold."

Wes maneuvered her body beneath the sheet and comforter and climbed in beside her.

Pleasure still raced through her veins and she tucked her arms up between them as he rubbed her back. "You're exquisite, Tabby Cat."

"Thanks," she sort of mumbled, and licked her lips. They were still a bit dry from the gag. "Mmm. The gag."

"Thought you'd like that. Fuck, you looked good in it."

"Mmm. Rope," she added on a sigh.

"You're rope drunk."

"And cock drunk." She laughed and relaxed against him.

For several minutes, they lay there and he ran his hands through her hair and across her back. And kissed her cheek.

It was nice.

But it wasn't what she needed.

And he wasn't who she wanted it from.

"Need some water?" he asked, startling her awake. "Sorry." He kissed her cheek. "Didn't mean to wake you."

"Didn't mean to fall asleep. Sorry. Haven't been sleeping all that well lately."

"Rope, blindfolds and orgasms. If more doctors knew what to prescribe, I bet people would go to them more often."

Tabitha stretched and rolled onto her back, deliciously sore. "Water would be great."

He got out of bed, heading into the bathroom.

She rubbed her eyes and glanced around again. Michael was most definitely still not there. "How long was I out?"

With a glass of water in hand, he headed back toward her. "Ten minutes or so, I think. Not long." He handed her the glass and pulled on clothes while she drained its contents. "More?" He nodded to the glass as he took it from her.

"Love some more. Thirsty, I guess."

He winked at her. "Have to replenish all the fluid you lost."

His easy demeanor after they had sex was one of the things she liked most about him. She didn't have to stroke his ego or act as if they had any kind of relationship other than what was on the surface, no matter how powerful he was in reality. It was just easy.

But she honestly wanted him gone. Not because he'd done anything wrong but because her emotions were too close to the surface.

Coming out of subspace was one thing. Being yanked out and thrust into a cesspool of disappointment was going to wreck her. She stared at the empty glass and tried hard not to panic.

"Where's Michael?" Wes asked. "I thought he was supposed to be here by now." He said it from the bathroom, nonchalantly, and she was glad he couldn't see her face.

She stared at her phone as if it was a bomb ready to go off.

"Running late?" It came out a question instead of an answer.

Why hasn't he texted?

Or called?

Something?

She and Wes had been involved, but she'd have heard it.

She held her phone in her lap as Wes came back in with more water.

Taking the glass from him, she then pushed a button on her phone and swiped the screen to get it to come up. It came up on Michael's text screen and her stomach dropped.

"Want me to stick around till he gets here?"

Tunnel vision sucked all of Tabitha's attention to her phone. Her subspace high shattered as she read the messages waiting for her.

The museum wants me to do two more buildings for them.
So amazing!
We're talking specifics now.
Running a little bit late.
Not too much longer… I hope.
Fuck, baby. They're still here. I feel horrible. And my phone's about to die.
A few things to finish up.
So sorry.

Wes touched her shoulder and she jumped, spilling some of water from the glass she still held.

Closer to tears than she'd been with anyone other than Michael, she shooed Wes out of the room. "It's fine. He'll be here in a minute or two, I'm sure." Faking it wasn't going to last much longer. The shakes set in and she didn't want him to touch her again or he'd know something was wrong.

Really wrong.

"Are you sure you're okay? The last thing I want to do is bail if you still need me here."

"I'm fine." *Totally not fine.* And it wasn't that she didn't need someone. She just didn't need him.

"If you're sure, then I'll go. I'll call you tomorrow to check on you. Okay?" He added the last word a few seconds later when she didn't respond.

"Mm-hmm. Tomorrow."

His eyebrows turned low into a vee, but he shouldered his bag and walked around to her side of the mattress. He kissed her head and she had to hold her breath to lock her muscles up tight and keep the tears in place.

"Bye, Tabby Cat."

She attempted a smile and added a bit of a wave.

He paused at the door for a second then he was gone.

Silence set off her panic.

Alone.

She was completely alone.

A submissive without her Dom.

A wife without her husband.

A friend without her other half.

What a terrifyingly empty place.

A dark place where fear and hurt and hopelessness snuck in to yank her down and drown her.

She hadn't heard the texts because she must have turned off the volume when she'd almost dropped it when Wes got there.

How do I answer him?

What do I say?

Before she lost her nerve, she called his cell. Straight to voicemail. More than likely dead with no charger at work. Pushing the end call button, she cut off his voice in the middle of a sentence.

That was how she felt.

Cut off in the middle of something amazing because he wasn't there.

She needed him and her protector wasn't there.

Tabitha sat there under the covers, leaning against the headboard, trying to figure out what to text. Nothing. She had nothing.

She had no clue how long she sat there staring at the screen. Long enough for it to go black.

She set her phone down and reached for her water.

Work. She could call him at work. But what would she say?

A knock on the hotel room door startled her.

Joy lifted her spirits and she bolted to the door. Then she had a moment of self-preservation and grabbed a blanket off the bed to wrap around herself.

Excitement raced through her.

Michael made it!

The ping-pong of emotions made her a bit nauseous but it didn't matter. Nothing mattered but getting to the man she'd given herself to years ago. Nothing mattered but him.

She shoved the latch aside, unlocked the door and yanked it open.

Her smile died on her face as Wes stared back at her.

"I know something's wrong and couldn't just leave when you were upset. Did Michael already get here?" He leaned to the side to look around the room.

She tried to think of something to say.

Tried to come up with anything to hide her devastation because Michael wasn't there.

Instead, she buried her face in the blanket. The emotions she'd kept at bay hauled her beneath the black surface of fear and swallowed her whole.

Chapter Nine

Wesley

"Whoa, whoa, whoa. Tabby Cat, What's wrong?" He shut the door behind him and scooped her up.

She tucked her head into his neck and cried. She tried to speak but could only sob.

His heart squeezed in his chest at how upset she was.

A heart he'd long thought immune to sentiment.

He'd never seen her anything but happy and bubbly. The difference was startling and he wanted to nuke whatever had brought her to tears.

To his car to put his bag inside was as far as he'd made it. Leaving her, knowing she was upset by something, just hadn't worked for him. So he'd come back up. By the looks of her, it was good he had.

Sitting in one of the side chairs, he held her close and let her cry it out. He whispered to her, telling her it would be okay. And he believed every word. Because if it was in his power, he'd fix it, whatever it was. Tabitha was a rare kind of person.

Genuine.

What people saw was what people got. Including him.

Growing up the way he did, with the family name he had, and the amount of wealth preceding him, he tended to get a lot of hangers-on. So when people like Tabitha came into his life and cared about *him*, he wanted to hold on as hard as he could.

When her tears finally slowed, she blew out one big breath.

He grabbed a tissue from a side table next to them and lifted her chin to dry below her eyes.

"I must look horrible," she grumbled and tried to take the Kleenex.

"Beautiful as always." He didn't rush and he wouldn't let her pull away until he was finished drying her cheeks. "Let's get you under some covers and then you're going to tell me what's going on. And only because you're so upset am I going to let that facial expression go without a punishment, so don't get used to it."

She attempted a smile but she didn't get very far.

Picking her up, he then set her on the bed. Soon, he had her beneath the covers, so he grabbed her glass of water and sat on the edge of the mattress.

After she took a drink, he set the glass on the nightstand then stared at her. "What's going on? And don't try to tell me anything other than the truth because I'm not leaving until I know what has you so upset."

She rubbed her lips together. "I don't want to talk about it. I just want everything to go back to the way it was." More tears slipped over her lashes and she quickly brushed them away.

"The way what was?"

"My marriage."

Dread dropped into the pit of Wes' stomach. "He was supposed to be here, wasn't he?"

She nodded and glanced at the clock. "Two hours ago. He was supposed to be here two hours ago. He knew about the date and promised he would be here to put me back together. He promised but he got held up at work. Again."

Anger lit inside Wes, though he had no right to dictate who she wanted with her for aftercare. He tamped down the urge to growl since he wasn't her man. His best friend was her man and he damn well knew it.

He'd never wanted to be anyone's man, so the feeling was more than a bit foreign.

"And where is he now?"

She shrugged. "Still at the office, I guess." She shrugged. "I didn't text him back right after we got done. Didn't know what I wanted to say."

Sadness or something close to despair clung to her as if it were a heavy blanket, and he wasn't certain she could bear the weight of it.

He'd never seen her sad before. Ever.

Scared? Sure. She was a nervous little thing when she didn't know what he had planned for her.

But sad? Never.

It was a travesty. Creatures such as her should never be sad, and for once he was pissed he wasn't the one to be able to fix it for her.

"I tried to call, but it went right to voicemail."

"I did, too, when I was on the way back up here."

"Phone probably died and he doesn't have the extra charger with him. I keep telling him to take to the office."

Her voice. So quiet.

Lost.

"Is this the first time he's missed something?"

She glanced up at him then down to her hands in her lap as she shook her head. "He missed a dinner earlier this week. Forgot."

"Forgot? That doesn't sound like Michael."

"I know. That's why I want my marriage back to what it was. Lately…" She shrugged again. "It hasn't been perfect."

Wes figured that was quite an understatement if she'd been reduced to tears that just wouldn't abate. Not to mention subdrop probably being a factor, but that wasn't anything he'd ever faced with her before.

"I'm sure he's probably on his way," she offered quietly. She didn't sound as if she believed it.

"Have you talked to him about all of this?"

She wiped another tear but a new one took its place. "I was going to talk to him tonight. After he got here. Finally got my nerve up to tell him this isn't working and we have to do something about it. How's that for irony?"

Wes grabbed her hand and gave it a squeeze. "Want me to hang out until he gets here? You being alone right now doesn't really sound like a great idea."

"You don't need to stay. I'll be fine. I'm just gonna wait here for him. Maybe grab food."

Which was probably a total lie, since she never ate when she was upset over anything.

She wiped her eyes and looked away. "Really, I'm fine."

"Don't hide from me, Tabby Cat."

"You seeing me upset is not one of my kinks."

"I'm pretty sure I can handle it." He brushed a tear away and fought the impulse to shed his clothing and crawl into bed next to her. But that reeked of a relationship, which they didn't have. Crossing that line when she was hurt and vulnerable would have made him the biggest asshole around. And he certainly wasn't going to complicate her life any more by developing some kind of romantic feelings for her.

Lustful? Hell, yes.

Plus, she was most definitely his friend, too, and *that* he could do something about. Namely, by going to talk some sense into her husband.

"Are you all right? Want me to draw you a bath before I go?"

"That would actually be really nice." A soft smile lifted her lips. "I'm sure my sore ass would second the notion."

He turned on the water and added soap to get her some bubbles. He flexed his hand. Talking to her over the water, he called out, "My palm might actually be a bit sore. I'll definitely have to switch my grip more next time." No answer came. Adjusting the water temperature, he stayed for just a few more seconds then glanced out to the bedroom. She had her phone to her ear. "Tabitha?"

She was quiet for a second and closed her eyes, pulling the phone away and pushing a button. "He called from work and left a message a few minutes ago. He still hadn't even left yet. The clients just walked out. He's sorry.

Again." She shook her head and tossed her phone onto the mattress. Climbing out of bed, she brushed another tear away. "Thank you very much for being awesome." She approached him and when she was close enough she got up on her tiptoes and kissed his cheek.

"But get out?" He filled in what she was probably too nice to say.

Trying to smile didn't come close when it couldn't reach her eyes. "That would be it. I don't think I'm going to be very good company." She took a step toward the bathroom but he caught her arm gently and pulled her close.

He hugged her tightly and rubbed her back softly. "You need me, you call me, understand?"

A mumbled answer came from her mouth but it wasn't coherent.

Pulling back a bit, he lifted her chin and stared into her wet eyes. "Understand, Tabby Cat? Doesn't matter the time of day or night. I'll take you over my knee before I go if you need a reminder of how I normally handle such matters."

A small smile softened her gaze for a moment. "No reminder needed. I'll call if I need to."

"Good girl." He kissed her forehead and let her pull away.

"Thanks for tonight, Wes. For everything."

"Always my pleasure. Before you get in the bath, lock the door behind me." Both of them headed toward the door and he made sure she was safely behind it before he opened it.

He felt the need to say something else, but there really wasn't anything to add. Not yet. Not until he got to Michael's office and figured out what was going on with him. He palmed Tabitha's cheek one last time and stepped through the open door. He waited long enough to hear the lock snick into place then he headed off down the hallway.

Poking his nose into other people's business wasn't something he made a habit of unless it was really important.

For Tabitha it was.

* * * *

Twenty minutes later, he walked into his best friend's office space, where he'd spent countless hours over the last two years poring over plans, designs and contracts.

Talk about a very different reason for opening the door. "You here?" Wes hoped Michael didn't answer. Hoped he was already on the way to the hotel. Or already there.

"In here," Michael called out from the direction of his office.

"Damn," Wes cursed under his breath. He stepped around the empty reception desk and toward the back. "I tried to call you," Wes said by way of greeting.

"Phone crapped out." He picked it up and tossed it back onto his desk. "I never got any response from Tabitha. Is she okay?" Wes could tell Michael already knew the answer.

"No."

"Fuck." He ran his hands through his hair and stared down at whatever he'd been working on.

"What was so important it couldn't wait until Monday? Or even tomorrow?" Wes tried to keep the anger out of his voice as he headed farther into Michael's office and took a seat.

"The museum deal. They could only meet today and I couldn't say no. A meeting that should have taken less than a couple hours turned into six because they want me to do two other buildings along with the main one now."

"That's great for business." And it was. Wes tried not to growl at the end.

"I broke a promise tonight."

He didn't hide stuff and he didn't pull punches. Another reason Wes liked doing business with him and trusted him with more than just his bottom line. "I wondered if it was something like that. Tabitha is..." *This is so not my forte.* "Super hurt. She counted on you and you weren't there. I'm not trying to bust your balls but I care about her. I've never seen her like that. You're my best friend, but, damn, man. Just…damn."

Michael hung his head. "It's like I have an angel and a devil on my shoulders lately. Both telling me what I need to be doing, but I just don't have enough hours in the day."

"One's not good and the other bad. Tabitha or work. Work or Tabitha. There's a happy medium in there. You just have to find it. Trust me. I know a lot about getting lost in work and everything else disappearing."

"My shitty father beat it into me. That I was worthless. Never going to amount to anything. I've pushed and pushed to prove him wrong. And to make Tabitha proud. To provide for us. Our future." He shook his head. "I really fucked up tonight."

They'd talked before about shitty fathers. Which was probably another reason why they were so close now. "Have you told her that?"

"What, that I fucked up? Yeah. Unfortunately, I've told her that a lot lately. A lot."

"No. That you're doing what you're doing so that she's proud of you. That she's still at the forefront of your mind even with all the late nights and early mornings."

"I'm sure she knows."

"Are you sure? Because if you haven't told her, I bet she doesn't have any clue why she's alone at your hotel right now wondering where you are. And that's just how I see it, looking in from the outside. Take it with a grain of whatever, but if I were you?" He pointed to his desk. "There is nothing more important than the woman I just left who is waiting for you."

"You're right. Completely right. And I really appreciate you coming all this way to say it to my face. A lot, man. I've had my head in the sand for a while, assuming everything would find its place again. It just isn't."

Wes nodded. "Life isn't that easy, unfortunately. Leaving to get to her at the hotel?" He glanced at his watch, knowing Michael still had a twenty-minute drive to get to the hotel if he left then.

"One last thing to send off and then I'm out. Then I don't have to come in tomorrow at all."

Wes stared at him as he flipped back and forth between two plans. He and Michael were very much alike when it came to business. Strong work ethic. Passionate. A belief that if one put the hours in then the clients would come, and it had worked for both of them. It make it harder because he understood Michael's need to finish what he'd started. To put everything to bed, so he could go fix his relationship with his wife.

He sure as hell wasn't going to judge the man for setting a goal and achieving it. But he wondered at what price he was willing to pay to make it happen. A very steep price if he really didn't get out of the office. And fast.

"Then I'll let you be so you can get done." He turned to go but stopped at the door. "One more thing." Apparently, he wasn't completely finished sharing the wisdom he could see so clearly from the outside looking in.

Michael raised his head and waited.

"Monogamy and I aren't on speaking terms. Never have been. But Tabitha? She'd make any man contemplate marriage." He smirked. "As much as anyone with our predilections can."

"What's that supposed to mean?" Michael's eyebrows dipped and he made a fist.

Wes shrugged. "Just what I said. You have a jewel among women in your possession. And I use the word possession very specifically. You don't have a collar around her throat but I believe the thoughts and feelings behind it are there. Don't lose what you have, reaching for something else. It won't be any good if you don't have her to share it with."

Wes opened the door and headed out. As it was closing, he heard Michael mumble, "I'll fix this. I have to."

He hoped he did, for all their sakes.

Chapter Ten

Michael

Less than thirty minutes later, Michael stood at the hotel door with flowers. Hyacinths. Tabitha's favorite.

Knock, knock, knock.

Regret roared through him. He'd fucked up. Bad. And he knew it.

On the way there, he reflected he should have called the hotel from his office phone but he hadn't thought of it soon enough.

Waiting for her to answer the door seemed to take forever. He looked up and down the hall but never saw anything or anyone else.

Never heard anything inside the room, either.

Nothing.

He checked the room number on the wall again. 420. Definitely the right one.

Knock, knock, knock, knock. "Tabitha? You in there?" he called out and tried the door. Locked of course.

Another minute went by, still nothing.

She might be in the bath. Could be. It was more than plausible. Yet apprehension filled his chest.

He took the elevator back down, heading to the front desk, where a woman in a suit did something on a computer. She looked up with a smile as he approached. "How can I help you?"

"I have a reservation for Graves. My wife already checked into room 420 but we need another key."

"No problem. Can I see some ID?"

Juggling the flowers made him very aware of them. He dug out his wallet and handed over his driver's license. Thankfully, Tabitha always put the room under both of their names.

She pushed more buttons on the computer.

 "Give me just a second, Mr. Graves." She handed back his license. "Let me just key another card for you and you'll be all set."

"Thanks." He wanted to ask if she'd seen Tabitha leave. He needed to ask if his wife had already checked out. He yearned to ask if she had a cell phone charger he could buy, but he didn't voice any of those questions.

He stood there and silently urged her to go faster.

What was either thirty seconds or three hours later, she slid the card into its little hotel-card condom and handed it over. "Enjoy your stay and let us know if you need anything else."

Out of habit, he called, "Thank you," over his shoulder as he walked away.

Retracing his footsteps back up to the room didn't take long. After sliding the card in and the little light above the handle blinked green twice, Michael twisted the handle and pushed it open. He called for her. "Tabitha? You here? I'm so sorry I'm so late. I know I fucked up. Tabitha?"

An eerie quiet was his only greeting.

Dread punched him in the gut when none of her stuff was on the luggage stand. Nothing beside the bed or in the bathroom.

Fuck.

Just nothing.

One of the beds looked as if it hadn't been touched. The other had definitely been used. He ground his teeth together. His wife had needed him and he hadn't been here.

In exasperation, he tossed the flowers down on the closest bed and they rustled a small piece of paper he'd missed on his first look around off the corner of the mattress.

With his heart in his throat, he picked up the note and

sank onto the edge of the bed. Before he flipped it over he already knew what was going to be on it.

A sad face drawn in the middle of the white piece of paper.

To anyone else, it probably wouldn't seem like much, but to Michael it was as if someone had pulled the pin on a grenade and tossed it to him.

Years before, when they first got together, he'd realized what a dickhead her ex was. Manipulating her emotions and making her think they were bad. Sometimes, early on, with sensitive subjects, they'd texted about them instead of talking. It had been easier for her to process, so she didn't panic. They'd texted a lot. And sometimes when he was at work or she was out with friends he'd give her a hard time if they were apart too long and he'd send her a sad face emoji.

Just something cute to tell her he was sad without her.

Months after he'd started doing it, she'd texted him from the other end of the couch. She'd told him how much it ripped her up inside when he sent her a sad face. She'd asked how he would feel if she sent one to him.

He told her he didn't know. He hadn't realized she'd never sent one back.

So she'd sent one.

Talk about horrible. He'd put his phone down and gathered her onto his lap. She'd shaken in his arms as he'd held her tight.

They'd agreed that night to never send a sad face unless things were really, *really* wrong.

He stared down at the sad face she'd left for him and his stomach turned over. Another thought struck him and his heart skipped a beat. If he'd already collared her his collar would be sitting with the note. No question.

The need to vomit or punch a wall built inside him.

What am I going to do?

"Home. She had to have gone home." Since she couldn't reach him through his dead cell phone, he was certain that's where she would be.

He grabbed the flowers, tossed the key card onto the nightstand and headed out.

* * * *

Less than ten minutes later he pushed open the door leading into the house from the garage. He glanced back at the spot she parked in.

The empty spot.

With his stomach tied in knots, he called for her. "Baby?" But he knew she wouldn't be there to answer.

He set the flowers on the counter. Next to another note.

Went to clear my head. Don't wait up.

First reaction?

To get pissed because he normally knew where she was any hour of every day.

Second reaction, very quickly on the heels of the first? Scared shitless because she hadn't run from him like that in years. From them. They worked things out. Always. No running. It was one of the biggest things he'd convinced her of when they got together. Especially when their BDSM relationship had developed. They could work anything out. Together.

He'd joked about it being a rule for years. Maybe he should have made it a real rule.

Wiping a hand down his face, he tried to think of where she'd go. Where he could follow her.

Then he remembered his cell.

He yanked it out of his pocket and moved to the counter where the charger was sitting. Plugging it in, he tried to power it on, but it was so dead it wouldn't do anything. "Dammit." Frustration bled from his pores and he wanted to hit something.

Racing to the bedroom, he took the stairs two at a time. He snatched the cordless phone off the nightstand and dialed

Tabitha's cell phone.

It rang.

Again.

And again.

So she could see he was calling and was ignoring him.

He blew out a weary breath as her voicemail picked up.

"Hi! This is Tabitha. Leave me a message and I'll call you back. Byyeeeeee."

Beep.

"Shit, Tabby. You aren't home. I know I fucked up." He shook his head. "I know I hurt you. Disappointed you. I'm so fucking sorry. Please come home. And don't run. We can work this out. Believe me. Please. Come home. I love you. So much." He didn't want to hang up. He pulled the phone away from his ear and just stared at it. It was almost as if it was his last connection to her. To sever it seemed... horrifying.

Brushing his thumb over the off button, he finally pushed it, unwilling to believe he wouldn't get a chance to make things right. He tossed the phone onto the bed behind him and put his head in his hands.

Things were much more desperate than he'd thought. He'd been unwilling to see how badly he'd been letting her down lately. And he'd knowingly been not mentioning how her eyes had been looking like they had when they'd first gotten together.

Guarded.

Weary.

"Where would you go, Tabby? Who would you — Robin!" He snatched up the phone and dialed their neighbors, uncaring how late it was. He stood up to pace while it rang. He was certain Tabitha had talked to her the other night but he hoped Robin would still talk to him. He prayed she knew something to help him find her.

"Tabitha?" Robin answered the phone and Michael already had his answer.

"No. It's Michael."

143

"Damn. I was hoping she took my advice and went home."

"She was here at some point, but she left again. Was counting on you knowing where she went so I could go get her. You don't know where she is, do you?"

"No. But she told me she's safe when she called about forty minutes ago."

"I fucked up so bad."

"Yes. You did." Robin was never one to sugarcoat anything. "She didn't give me specifics about what happened tonight, but I already knew things were off after you missed your meetversary dinner this week. So, right now? Whatever you did? Pretty much makes me want to come over there and kick you in the nuts. I won't. But I really want to."

Another punch to the gut, knowing Tabitha had talked to Robin about him fucking up lately. He pinched the bridge of his nose. *Talk about letting her down in epic proportions.*

"Just answer me one question," she demanded.

"Ready." Because he had nothing to lose.

"Are you fucking around on her?"

"Dear God, no. No! I would never do that. Ever. I haven't been interested in another woman since we got together. The thought of putting my dick in someone else makes me want to puke." As if he needed something else to tie his stomach in knots. "Fuck, I hope Tabitha doesn't think I'd do something like that."

"She doesn't. She told me the other night when I was there because I brought it up to her, too. What kind of friend would I be if I didn't ask the hard questions?"

He paced some more. "I would never betray her trust like that. Ever. She's the other half of me and mine to protect, and everything I've been doing lately is for us. So we can have a better life. A brighter future."

"Thank fuck. And I believe you. If I didn't, I'd already be down there to remove your balls."

"I'm gonna fix this, Robin."

"I know you will." She sounded sincere, which was more than he deserved. "And do you want to know how I know this?"

"How?" Because he honestly didn't know what he was going to do yet. Other than lots of praying until she got home, and a huge amount of apologies and groveling when she did.

"Because you love her. The real kind of love. The forever kind. And she loves you the same. She's not going to throw that away, and you won't let her go without a fight."

"She's my everything. I have no clue how I got so off-track."

"But you know you're off-track. That's half the battle. Did she text you anything about where she was going? She wouldn't tell me on the phone."

"It wasn't on the note on the counter. Don't know yet on my phone, but I hope so. My phone completely died and wouldn't come back on. It's charging downstairs. Hopefully when I go back down it'll power on. If she calls will you…" He ran out of steam before he could finish because he had so much to tell Tabitha and didn't know where to start. And he wanted to tell her in person. Not through someone else.

"If she calls, I'll let you know. If she wants company, I'll get to her. I don't think either of us really wants her alone at the moment."

"Thanks, Robin. A lot. I honestly wasn't certain if you'd talk to me or not."

"None of us are perfect. Most of us aren't even close. You and Tabitha belong together. You just do. It's how I feel about Roland. If there was more love in the world it would be a better place."

"I couldn't agree more."

"I'm gonna climb off my soapbox now. Let me know if she gets home and I'll do what I can on my end, too."

"Thanks. A lot."

"Welcome."

Michael pushed the end button and headed downstairs

to see if he could get his phone to work. He'd thought about doing it while he spoke to Robin but he was honestly worried of what he'd find. Something awful, or nothing at all.

Which is worse?

He didn't know.

Holding the power button, he didn't have to wait long. It took his phone less than two seconds to blink on.

Everything started initializing quickly.

Several missed call notifications popped up. One from Wes and two from Tabitha. Something else he'd failed her at. He looked down at the other charger she'd bought for him to take to work. He just hadn't done it yet. *Later*, he'd thought several times.

Just doing it could have saved him hours of worry now. *Too busy?* He'd truly not taken it because of the piss poor excuse of being too busy? He shook his head.

Text notifications lit up his screen. Scrolling through, there were several from clients, a couple from Wes and two from Tabitha.

He had to lean against the counter because they knocked the wind out of him.

The oldest? A sad face.

But not an emoji. Not a silly yellow face with a frown.

No.

It was a selfie of Tabitha, tear tracks down her cheeks.

He couldn't think of another time she'd sent him a picture like that. And he vowed never to give her a reason to send another one.

The second text?

He stared at the clock.

Twelve minutes ago. Probably sent when he was on with Robin.

Got your message. Love you, too. Just don't know how to feel about the rest of it right now. I'm overwhelmed. Turning off my phone. Need some space to sort some things out. I'll let you know where I end up if I don't come home tonight.

That was it, and he was thankful for what she'd sent, though it made him want to dig a deep, deep hole for himself to contemplate things in.

He quickly sent her a reply.

Be safe. Please. That's all I ask. I'll be here when you're ready to come home.
I love you more than anything.

He glanced at her note again.

Yes, he would definitely be waiting up. It didn't matter when she got in. He wouldn't sleep until he knew she was safe. Safe in his arms. Exactly where she belonged.

He unplugged the cable and took that upstairs with him so the phone could charge while he took a shower. And if he couldn't calm down afterward he'd grab his keys and go look for her. She'd asked for space and he wanted to give her that, but he'd already failed her once. What if something happened to her while he wasn't there to protect her?

He shook his head and choked the cord in his grasp.

What kind of husband would he be if he let that happen?

What kind of Dom to the most precious thing in his world?

His fault. This was his fault and he had to fix it.

Hours spanned before him to contemplate everything he stood to lose if Tabitha left for good. He sent up another prayer to keep her safe.

The rest of his life would start when she walked back through their door, and he had some things to put into perspective so he could be the husband she needed him to be again.

The Dom she deserved.

There was a saying he'd heard countless times before. *You don't know what you've got till it's gone,* but he knew exactly what he had.

Perfection.

And he wasn't giving up on them without a fight.

Chapter Eleven

Tabitha

Tabitha stared at her phone as it powered off and the dark room she sat in closed all around her.

A part of her felt as if she'd amputated something vital keeping her alive.

A fundamental piece.

A section of her heart, maybe.

Something she needed to survive, but it hurt too bad to keep on life support.

Never. Not once in their marriage had she consciously turned her phone off to keep from talking to Michael.

Not once.

She'd run before. Years ago. But she'd always kept the lines of communication open and she'd always told him where she was going. That probably didn't constitute running away, but it was enough to give her a little while to find her balance again.

He'd always been a lifeline to her. Her safety net.

But now?

She tucked her phone into her purse and set it on the receptionist's desk in front of her.

Graves Design and Construction.

That was where she'd run to.

Ironic, she thought.

Tabitha figured it was the last place he would think to look even though he had cameras covering all angles of the building inside and out. She didn't want to be out in the open.

Exposed.

Vulnerable.

With no one to watch her back.

Reaching up, she then gripped the back of her neck, trying to relieve the headache that had settled in hours before. Attempting to alleviate the pain seemed to be a thankless job.

In the dark, she closed her eyes and tried to block out... everything.

The hurt of not being important enough anymore.

The fear of what she would have to talk about when she finally went home.

The shame of knowing she could have avoided what had happened tonight if she'd been stronger and talked to Michael before her date.

Rubbing her temples didn't help. The shame crept in anyway.

The thought of taking some ibuprofen and having some tea crossed her mind but actually walking all the way back to the kitchen seemed insurmountable.

She had no idea how long she sat there. No clue what she really thought about. Just an endless loop of 'what-if's and 'what went wrong's.

She kept trying to tell herself what happened wasn't that big a deal.

But it was.

It just...was.

Sitting at the desk facing the front door, she watched Robin walk up to the tinted glass wall in front of her. Her best friend cupped her hands around her eyes and leaned close to the glass. Robin cocked her head to the side. Then the other side. Searching for Tabitha.

Tabitha sat there and closed her eyes, not hiding, but not revealing herself, either. Maybe she'd go away. Maybe she wouldn't. Tabitha wasn't certain which one she wanted.

"I know you're in there, even though I can't see you. I saw your car." Robin paused for a second. "You might as well let me in. You have to know I'm not leaving you here alone."

Hiding behind the desk indefinitely crossed her mind, but the possibility of Robin walking away, leaving her alone again, scared her more.

She got up and trudged to the door.

Robin backed up when she saw her, waited for her to unlock the glass door, then pulled it open.

Locking it again fell to Robin this time. Then she pulled Tabitha into a big hug.

Tabitha held on with her head on Robin's shoulder and waited for the tears to come.

Nothing.

Nothing came.

She'd apparently done a very thorough job of shoving her emotions down good and deep after she'd lost it in front of Wes.

Broke down in front of the man who'd just fucked the shit out of her.

Tabitha shook her head and pulled away.

"What?" Robin asked her.

"I cried tonight."

"I would think so."

"No." Tabitha wiped a hand down her face and rubbed her eyes. "I cried in front of Wes. God, it was so embarrassing."

"Girls cry. Guys know this. He'll survive." Robin grabbed her hand and led her back through the offices to the kitchen, turning a few small lights on as they went. Thankfully, she'd been there at the grand opening and several other times so she knew her way around.

Tabitha wasn't focusing very well and wasn't going to be much help.

A plastic bag Tabitha hadn't noticed when she came in hung on Robin's arm. Robin set it on the counter and opened it up.

"What do you have?" Tabitha asked as she took a seat at the small table against the far wall.

"Reinforcements."

"What kind?"

"The chocolate kind and the funny movie kind."

"You really are a great best friend, you know that?"

"I know." She winked at her and set out to make tea. Tea she'd brought with her. Tabitha's favorite peppermint tea. Even her favorite brand.

At that, Tabitha teared up.

She piled her hands on the table and put her forehead on top. Partially to hide, partially because the top of her head was going to explode at any time.

A few minutes later, Robin rubbed her back, and a mug *tinked* against the table as she set it down. "Here. Take this."

Tabitha lifted her head and wiped a couple of tears from her cheeks.

A box of Kleenex sat in the middle of the table and Robin handed her ibuprofen and a small glass of water.

"How'd you know?"

"We both get headaches when we're up too late. Figured yours would be doubly awful with being upset."

"You're so awesome." Tabitha took the meds and washed them down.

"Now drink some tea and let me get some water before we chat."

Tabitha handed over her glass and pulled the mug toward her.

Robin set her glass in the sink and poured another glass from the water cooler right inside the door. "I've been so thirsty all day. I obviously didn't drink enough water after dinner with Roland tonight."

"Oh, fuck," Tabitha cursed.

"What?"

"Roland is back. You came here when he just got home. You should go. Be with him. Oh, my God, I'm so sorry, I didn't think when you showed up—"

"Breathe. It's fine. He's got some wicked jet lag and fell asleep an hour before I figured out where you probably were. I left him a note, but he won't be up again until tomorrow. And even if he was, leaving you to deal with all of this on your own didn't do it for me."

"But he's been gone for a week."

"And we had sex for nearly three hours after my awesome cooking class this morning."

"Oh," was all Tabitha could cough up on short notice.

"So, everything is fine for me to be here. And even if he'd just gotten home, I'd have explained the situation and I'd still be here. We stick together." She put her hand on top of Tabitha's and smiled. "And I'm still wooing you to be my slave."

A small smile tilted Tabitha's lips and she stared into her tea mug. "Well, there is that."

Robin grasped her hand a little tighter until Tabitha looked up at her.

It was a rare occasion when her best friend was serious. In the years since they'd met, it had happened less than a handful of times.

She added one more time to the tally as Robin's green-eyed gaze bored into hers.

When she was serious, everyone paid attention.

"I am so lucky to have you as my best friend. I wouldn't be here if it wasn't for you and we both know it."

"That's not tru—"

"It is. When I..." Robin trailed off, and it seemed as if she was having to swallow her own emotions to continue. "Miscarried, you found me. You got the paramedics there. You saved me. I would have died if you hadn't come to check on me."

Tabitha wiped new tears from her cheek. "I've told you so many times before. It could have been nothing more than a coincidence."

"I don't believe that. Never will. And I don't think you do either. You say all the time that it was fate we met. It most certainly was. You're like my fairy godmother. We'd only known each other for, what? Three months at that point?

Everything happens for a reason. And you were there with me for the whole recovery. Right beside Roland. Even when I lost my shit you were right there."

"My heart broke for you. I wouldn't let you go through that alone."

Robin tilted her head to the side. "I couldn't have said it better myself. You being anywhere alone tonight was just not an option. I know you said you wanted to be by yourself, but that wasn't really going to work for me."

"Thanks. I didn't think I wanted any company, but I do."

"Speaking of company, have you told Michael where you are? I talked to him on the phone earlier. He was really worried."

Tabitha took another drink of tea and hoped the ibuprofen would kick in soon. "I texted him and told him I was okay. Didn't tell him where I was. The idea of having to talk all of this out right now..." She shook her head. "Just not something I can handle. Just. Not." She chewed the inside of her cheek. "You talked to him?"

"I did. He called the house looking for you."

"I love that he thought I'd be there. Which is one of the reasons I didn't want to go to your place. But I love that he checked."

"So, I have a question," Robin told her. "Do you want me to be the 'men are all pigs and they need to croak a painful death of a thousand suns' friend or the 'I'm gonna give you my opinion because I love you so much' friend?"

"Is asking for some kind of combo platter an option?"

"Of course." Robin exaggerated the last word. "Okay. Wait, wait. We need chocolate." She got up, grabbed the bag and sat back down. "I brought milk chocolate, dark chocolate and peanut butter cups. Figured I'd cover all my bases. Pick your poison."

"Yes," Tabitha answered.

Robin laughed and opened everything. "Another reason why we're destined to be besties till we're old with blue hair, telling people to get off our lawns."

"Looks like you're already ahead of the curve on the blue hair part."

She glanced up and smiled. "Forgot it's a blue stripe now. I love changing the color. It's always a rainbow kind of surprise when I look in the mirror." After pushing the packages between them, Robin broke off part of the milk chocolate bar.

Tabitha opted for a peanut butter cup.

"Now, we're ready. Okay. Guys can suck it on occasion. Seriously, they can be great and then all of a sudden their assholian tendencies crop up and reiterate to the world they can be complete douchebags."

"So true."

"Just you wait, missy. I'm only getting started. I know they're supposed to be completely evolved and walk on two legs and all that jazz, but you know what? They are men, from long lines of men. Hunters and gathers and the predisposed genetic half of our population who need to take care of their families. Not need as in I need another piece of chocolate, but need as in this is the sole purpose of their lives. And Michael is like Roland in this regard. It's a large part of him to work and provide for you."

"But I work too. We share all of our responsibilities, chores, money making."

"Agreed. In kink, do you switch?"

Tabitha probably got a bit of whiplash staring over at Robin. "What?"

"Just answer the question? Which side of the slash do you sit on? Or do you straddle both sides of it?"

"I don't top or dominate. Not at all. It's not my thing at all."

"And would you say Michael is the same? He's only on the other side? He's a top, a dominant, and could never be submissive?"

"Completely, yes. He doesn't have a submissive bone in his body."

"Exactly. He is dominant through and through. Everything

he does, everything he thinks, runs through that dominant brain of his. That hard-wired part of his noggin is thinking *Take care of my girl*. Being successful and taking care of his most precious possession, you, is his primary goal. Protect. My. Property."

"But I'm not his property. Not really."

"How do you figure?"

Tabitha glanced at Robin's throat where her collar sat. It wasn't a traditional collar but it was a collar nonetheless. "No collar. Not owned. And he didn't take care of me. He didn't show up. He wasn't there when I needed him."

Fuck.

Boom.

Actually saying the words rocked the foundation Tabitha was standing on. But she'd said them. She'd actually said them, all of them, and the world didn't end. It didn't come crashing down all around her. And she was still standing. Figuratively speaking.

" — really that black and white?" Robin had said something but Tabitha had missed it.

Tabitha shook her head. "Sorry, what was that?"

"I agree with you, he royally fucked up by not showing up tonight when he was supposed to. And, no, you don't wear a collar, but have you told him how much it would mean to you? How much it would help you feel safe? Can you expect him to just know these things? Is it really that black and white?"

"What do you mean?"

"Just like we talked before. He's not out cheating. He's not even out partying with his friends or getting drunk or high or anything heinous. Working to provide for both of you is what he was doing. It doesn't excuse what he did, but it's very different from those other things it could have stemmed from."

"I agree," Tabitha granted. "Which is why I haven't said anything for the past few months. I know what he's doing is noble and wonderful, but if I don't feel emotionally safe and connected to him I can't function."

"Which is exactly what you need to talk to him about." Robin paused and made a face as if she'd sucked on a lemon. "Okay. Don't hate me, but what I'm about to say is totally awful and somewhat judgmental. I'm gonna ask it, anyway. Why not stop being a hot wife? If that wasn't a factor, would everything else be easier if not disappear?"

"Being a hot wife had nothing to do with him missing our dinner on Thursday."

"True."

"And I've thought about that. A lot. Being a hot wife is part of who I am. It's part of our marriage and who we are as a couple. If we stop because we aren't interested in doing it any more that's one thing. If we stop because he can't make it a priority and lets me down then that changes us, our dynamic. Punishing both of us and changing our kink into something to resent isn't a workable plan either."

"Agreed. Just wanted to make sure you'd thought through all of the angles." Robin blew out a rough breath. "This thing we call marriage is a two-way street fraught with amazing things and heartache. Not to mention throwing BDSM and kink and a power exchange dynamic into the mix. But if we're lucky, this journey we're walking together? We'll always be going in the same direction. You have to tell him what you need. You have to discuss with him what's important to you."

"But he's always known in the past."

"Is that really fair to him? Or you?"

Tabitha absentmindedly licked chocolate off her fingers. "No. I guess it's not."

"We all change. 'For better or worse' wasn't just a phrase thrown in to fluff up the wedding vows. Marriage is work. It just is. But I'd honestly hate it if it were always easy." Robin shrugged and took a drink of her water. "Makes the great stuff so much more amazing when we work to get there. We make it happen when it's important. And he may not know how much you still rely on him, he may not know he's been letting you down because you haven't said anything to you. Maybe he's even noticed your little rule bending but didn't want to rock the boat so he didn't say anything."

"Well...damn. I never ever thought of it that way." Maybe, just maybe, Robin was right and they still had more common ground to find their way back to each other. Tabitha sure hoped so, because life without Michael in it was no life at all.

"Give it some thought. Take a deep breath before you talk to him, and speak from the heart. You both deserve to fix this. You're some of my favorite people in the whole world." Robin yawned. "Oh, and if we need to teach him a lesson in showing up for dates I know people who can bring the fiery pain of a thousand volcanoes."

"Good to know." Tabitha tried to smile but it felt forced. "Let's get out of here. It's late and you need to get home to your man."

"But we could stay and watch a movie if you wanted to." She dug in the bag. "I brought a wide variety, depending on what you were in the mood for. *Scream*, *Fried Green Tomatoes*, *Mary Poppins* and *The Exorcist*."

"Uhh..."

"I know, right? Totally covered every genre with those four. I killed it."

"We only have one problem."

"Which is what? No popcorn?" She pointed in the corner. "There's a bag right there."

"No player."

"D'oh. Dammit. I meant to bring my laptop and then I totally forgot. Shitballs."

Tabitha patted her arm and got up to pour out the tiny bit of tea at the bottom of her cup and rinse it out. "How about a movie night raincheck?"

"You're on, sister." Robin stood and pulled her in for another hug. "I'm here for you, you know that, right? Anything you need and I'm already there."

Emotions rose again and threatened to choke her words. Tabitha swallowed and cleared her throat. "I know, and can't tell you what it means to have you."

"Same goes. And I'll send the rest of the chocolate home with you. A little extra stash of therapy does every girl good."

They grabbed everything and turned the lights off as they left.

Pretty soon they were outside and Tabitha locked the front door again.

"Who's that?" Robin asked.

Tabitha turned around and stared as blood pumped harder through her system. "Is it…?"

A third car sat parked next to their two. They both paused by the front of the building when the door to the other vehicle opened and a man got out. Hoodie up, running pants, running shoes.

The man pushed the hoodie off his head.

"Wes," Tabitha breathed out as she deflated. "I was worried it was Michael even though I didn't know the car."

"I can imagine," Robin told her as they walked toward the line of cars.

"I wasn't about to leave two beautiful ladies on their own this late at night."

He hugged Tabitha when she was close enough, then waved at Robin.

He looked Tabitha over from head to toe. "You okay?"

"Hey, I'm gonna get out of here," Robin interjected. "That all right with you?" She stared at Tabitha with a whole lot of 'whatever you need' written in her expression.

"Yes, more than fine. Thank you." Tabitha hugged her close. "For everything."

"Welcome. Call me tomorrow…err…later today, and let me know if you need anything." She yawned again.

"I will."

"You gonna go home when you and Wes are done talking?"

"Yes," Wes answered for her.

"Maybe," she answered for herself with a roll of her eyes.

Robin laughed and hugged her one last time. "Just be safe. Promise?"

"Of course."

A couple of minutes later Robin's taillights were all Tabitha could see.

"How'd you know to find me here?" she asked Wes when they were alone.

"Nice deflection. I logged into Michael's cameras to make sure everything was locked up. I was hoping he left in a rush."

"You didn't tell him I was here, did you?" The question came out in a rush and her heart kicked into high gear. She couldn't help but look around Wes to peer in the passenger seat.

"No." He lifted her chin, forcing her to meet his eyes again. "I figured you could use a little time to get your bearings."

"Yeah." *Understatement of the year.* "I'm glad you're here, actually. I wanted to apologize. For earlier. I hated losing it in front of you. Seriously. I am so sorry."

His eyes narrowed. "If we were in any kind of appropriate location I would tan your ass red."

"For apologizing?"

"Yes."

"But—"

"No buts. That you are emotional is one of the main reasons I enjoy playing with you so much. You're electric and your emotions are one of the sexiest things about you. Yes, that's the first time I've truly seen you upset, but it's not the first time I've seen you cry."

"You whipping me with your belt until I cried is hardly the same thing."

"You're right. They are incredibly different, but it's still a peak of emotion. It's raw and real and authentic."

"I was afraid you'd avoid me from here on out because I lost my shit."

"You didn't lose your shit. You cried. You're allowed to be upset. It's permissible for you to not be okay when something hurts or upsets you. It sucks that Michael was the one who upset you, but I hate to break it to you…"

"Hate to break what to me?" Tabitha's heart stopped and she held her breath.

"We aren't infallible. Guys in general, or dominant types. We mess up."

Tabitha deflated and put her forehead on his chest.

He chuckled and rubbed her back. "I know. I blew your mind there."

"It's not that exactly." She straightened and gazed up at him. "And I know you guys aren't perfect. Nobody's perfect."

"No. We're far from perfect, but there's something else that I think you need to understand. Especially coming from a Dom's perspective."

"I'm all ears." And she was. She had no idea what he was going to say, especially since he rarely let her into his head.

"A submissive being disappointed in us is our greatest failure and our greatest fear."

Tabitha stared at him, trying to absorb all of the things that realization touched on. "I have no idea how to respond to that. That affects…"

"Everything. Everything we do, everything we are. It's one of the biggest driving forces in our lives. So when you talk to Michael, remember that."

"I will."

"You look dead on your feet, Tabby Cat. Let's get you in your car and on the way home. Unless you're too tired, and then I'll just take you home, and I can arrange for your car to be delivered later today."

"No, I'm good. Think I might drive around a little bit. I don't know if I'm ready to go home yet."

"Then don't mind me if I tail you at a mostly non-stalkerish distance."

Tabitha let out a little laugh and unlocked her door.

"There she is," Wes joked as he opened her door and helped her in. Then he blew out a breath. "I'll be going out of town in a few days. Don't know when I'll be back, but you can reach me on my cell anytime if you need me."

"Everything okay?"

"Time will tell."

Even for him, that was a cryptic answer. "This won't be the last time I see you, will it? Surely you're not going to be busy the next time I text for a date?" Nothing like a bit more panic to wake her back up.

Something in his gaze was off before he answered. Sad, maybe. "If I can say yes to anyone in the future then know it will most definitely be you." He winked at her and closed her door before she could respond.

Talk about a strange kind of goodbye.

He got in his car, started it and backed up to wait for her. She sat there for a second and finally started her vehicle.

Two-thirty.

In the morning.

A yawn overtook her whole body and she shook at the end.

No wonder she was so tired.

She closed her eyes for a second and sent up a little prayer of thanks for her amazing friends. She was blessed in so many ways.

She backed out of her parking space, then drove out of the lot, accelerating onto the highway with Wes about a hundred feet behind her.

His presence helped her breathe a bit more easily as she got on the highway.

She'd head toward home and go from there.

Her head was fuzzy from emotions and the headache but she knew they had to fix this.

Together.

She and Michael would fix it together.

"For better or worse," she mumbled to herself. "Nobody said it would be easy. For better or worse."

Chapter Twelve

Tabitha

Exhaustion clung to Tabitha when she opened the door to their house. It was late. Really late. As in, the sun was trying to peek over the horizon. She felt as if she'd been up for days.

She'd driven around for another hour before coming home. Uncertainty turned her stomach.

Thank goodness for it still being the weekend, because she sorely needed it. Having to go to work with the weight of the world on her shoulders would have made the situation unbearably worse.

If that could be possible.

She closed the door to the garage, feeling panic in her own house as she stepped inside. She felt uncomfortable. Unsafe. Not physically. Michael would never hurt her. *But the emotional stuff? Yeah.*

Leaving the house had made her feel safe for a second or two, but she didn't want to throw everything away, no matter how hurt she was. She'd needed a little space so she'd just gotten back in the car and left. No destination in mind. Her car had just kind of steered itself to Michael's office. She'd just wanted to clear her head. Find some answers.

But nothing had changed.

Nothing was answered.

Nothing remained but the hurt and fatigue. She'd told Michael she was safe on the text.

Safe was relative, as she stood on a very narrow fence. Alone.

Her friends were there for her but that was…different.

The man she belonged to, collar or not, hadn't been there, which had shattered any feeling of real safety.

She took a deep breath and second-guessed her decision not to stay at the hotel. She could still go back. Check out at noon then figure stuff out. But she didn't want to do that. Didn't want to be away from home.

Away from Michael?

She didn't want that, either. Not really.

But the clinging disappointment weighed her down, making her head foggy and her emotions raw.

The light beneath the microwave was on but nothing else. Beside the stove sat a vase of flowers. She stared at it, erecting another wall to keep herself safe until she could process her emotions again.

The thought of Michael being up waiting for her had run through her head for the past couple of hours. She knew they were going to have to talk, but the idea of having to rehash everything when she was already so tired made her eyes fill with tears.

She squeezed her eyelids closed and exhaled again, trying desperately for some kind of serenity.

Attempting to be quiet, she set her purse down on the counter along with the bag from Robin and hung her keys on the little hook by the coffee machine. Indecision swamped her. She wanted a shower and food and a hug and —

Light flooded the kitchen and mixed emotions erupted inside her.

Sadness and thankfulness and a more than a little bit of panic.

She turned around.

Michael stood in nothing but boxers on the other side of the kitchen that led into the living room. His hand was still on the light switch as he stared at her. His eyes were bleary, his hair mussed as if he'd been tossing and turning.

"Thank God you're home," he whispered.

Relief morphed into regret as he lowered his arm.

His muscles bunched as if he was going to step toward her, but then he relaxed.

Silently leaving the decision of the next step up to her spoke volumes. He knew things were bad. He knew.

As she'd driven home, she'd worried about how she would feel when she saw him.

Weary?

Sad?

Or something worse.

Nothing at all?

That was her most awful fear.

"Baby, I'm so sorry. I know it's not enough. I know it's not good enough for what I did, but…" He rubbed a hand over his hair and shook his head. "I'm just so sorry."

Emotion expanded between them at his simple apology. Remorse filled the room and Tabitha closed her eyes.

When she saw him, she wanted to be able to just say it was okay and move on. The need to brush it all away and bury it held so much pull she considered it for about two seconds. Wanting their connection forged again overpowered everything else.

Tears filled her eyes, slipping over her lower lashes.

"Oh, baby." Michael exhaled the words as if his heart were ripping in two. He pressed forward, eating up the distance between them.

She opened her arms to him a second before he got to her. He wrapped his arms around her waist to lift her against his chest was exactly what she'd wanted. Exactly what she'd needed tonight when she'd driven around trying to find some kind of understanding. Forgiveness?

Sorrow swamped her, sucking her under, into a place she didn't want to acknowledge. A dark space she'd been skirting for a lot longer than she'd been willing to admit.

Alone.

That was where she'd been for days. Weeks. Months.

Racking sobs broke free as Michael swayed with her back

and forth.

"I'm so sad," she mumbled past her tears as she buried her face in his neck and held on tighter. The tears came faster and she couldn't stop them. She tried so hard to clamp off the hurt but the unbidden pain tore out of her.

As if a floodgate had been released, the tears took over, drowning everything else in their path.

"I've got you, my love. I've got you." He scooped her up behind the knees and cradled her inside his embrace.

They moved, but she didn't know in which direction. Her eyelids were squeezed so firmly she didn't know if he'd turned off the light.

Then he took the stairs toward their master suite. He didn't stop until he was in the bathroom, but he didn't set her down.

Sitting with her in his lap on the side of the big tub, he reached over a bit and turned on the water. She held on tightly, unwilling to let go until he turned the water off. Her sobs quieted but the tears wouldn't stop.

He stood in silence and gently set her on her feet as she relaxed her hold around his neck.

Quietly, he undressed her, then grabbed a clip she had hooked on the side of their towel rack. He twisted her hair up and secured it, then lifted her into the bath. Quickly he stripped off his boxers and stepped into the tub behind her.

He sank into the water and pulled her back against his chest. Bathing together had been something they used to do all the time. Just one more thing that had gone by the wayside when life got in the way.

Turning to the side, she rested against him and took a deep breath.

"Good girl. And another." He inhaled slowly, encouraging her to do the same.

She tried.

Good girl. She didn't feel like a good girl.

More tears tumbled free and mixed with the warm water.

"I hate feeling weak," she whispered, and her bottom lip

trembled.

"You are *not* weak, Tabby. Not at all." Michael shook his head against her hair and lifted her chin to look down at her. "You're stronger than I am."

She opened her mouth to tell him how wrong he was and he kissed the words from her lips.

"It's true and you can't argue the point."

"But you—"

He kissed her again. "You've gone how long trying to handle this alone? Months?" He pulled her close to his chest again. "I've almost lost my shit a million times over these last few months and that was with your complete support. I barely made it through. You wreck me with how you've loved me. No, Tabby. You are not weak, do you hear me? You're so much stronger than I am it's not funny."

Brushing tears from her cheek, she closed her eyes. "I don't feel strong right now."

"You don't have to be. I'm here. I've got you. We'll get through this."

"Promise?" It was out before she thought about what she was saying. New tears welled over her lids and she shut her eyelids tight to keep from bawling again. She almost didn't want him to answer.

"On my life, I promise. God, I'm sorry."

They stayed in the tub, clinging to each other as Michael splashed water along her back and exposed shoulder to keep her warm.

Soon her eyelids grew heavy and she nodded off.

Michael woke her with kisses to the top of her head. "I don't want you getting cold. Let me get you out and dried off. I'll put you to bed. I'll—take the couch if you don't want me there."

She shook her head and tried to speak. It took her two tries to clear her throat so she could tell him, "Don't leave me. Being alone in our bed is the last thing I want."

He closed his eyes, nodded as if in prayer, and held her close for a few more seconds.

Tabitha stood as Michael steadied her and they stepped out.

Wrapping her up in a towel first, he dried her off then got one for himself. He pulled the plug to drain the tub and she brushed her teeth.

She got into bed and Michael pulled the curtains in their bedroom to block out some of the morning glow.

She stared at the sliver of light shining between the fabric and for some reason she couldn't look away. Something unexpected filled her chest with the dawning of a new day.

Hope.

Michael climbed into bed behind her, moving in close to spoon her body as she stared at the bright reminder that today was brand new and it would be what they made it.

As he tried to pull her close, she twisted around to face him.

Meeting his gaze was difficult, but each journey started with a single step.

She sank her teeth into her bottom lip as she tried to decide what to say. Trying to sleep with no real words between them wouldn't do. Anxious sleep was worse than no sleep at all.

"What, baby?" He used his fingertips and traced her cheeks, her nose, her lips. "Talk to me. Yell at me. Whatever you need."

"I want to talk tomorrow morning. Well, later this morning, when we wake up. I want to tell you what's bothering me and I want you to talk to me. I know not talking tonight goes against all the fibers in your being, but I just can't do it tonight. I honestly have nothing left for that conversation. That okay?"

A small smile lifted the corners of his lips. "I thought about pushing it. Thought maybe if I explained why I've been absent so much it might make it better. But it's not my call. Not by a long shot. If you need to sleep first so we can fix this then that's what we're going to do."

Tabitha just stared at her husband. She cupped his cheek

and kissed him. Scooting up in bed to get at a better angle, she then kissed him again. And again. "You have the softest lips I've ever kissed," she whispered against his mouth as she kissed him again, sliding her hand to the back of his neck to hold him closer. "And I love your scruff. Have I ever told you that before?"

His hands on her naked flesh sent tingling sensations everywhere he touched. Her hip, her waist, her back. "I think you may have mentioned something like that before. But you're wrong on one thing. Yours are much softer." Tugging her shoulders, he pulled her close so he could kiss her.

He touched his mouth to hers, kissing and loving her.

She opened to him and slid her tongue between his lips.

Michael's cock jerked against her abdomen and a tiny moan passed between them. Tabitha liked not knowing who made the noise. He reached behind her knee, pulling her leg between his.

"I want to do a different kind of talking."

"What kind?" he asked then kissed her again.

"I want to make love to you," she whispered.

He paused and tilted her head back a tiny bit to look into her eyes. "Are you sure, baby?"

Staring at him, she saw the man she married. The same man she'd trusted with her heart years ago, and she wanted to show how much she needed him. "I've never been more sure of anything in my whole life."

He stared back at her, love in his eyes. "Nothing would make me happier than making love to you."

She smiled and moved to straddle his hips. "You can have your turn in a minute." She settled above him, then reached between them and grasped his stiff cock. "Right now?" Rubbing the head of his cock along her slit made her wet and needy. "Right now, I'm going to make love to you. I need it."

"Fuucckkkk," he groaned as she lowered herself down onto him.

Their connection slipped into place.

She'd missed it after being with other men. She knew that. Had already admitted it was something she desperately needed. But she hadn't acknowledged half of her need for him.

Perfection had nothing on how right Michael felt inside her.

Her sex sheathed his hard length and he grabbed her hips, holding her in place. "Wait a second. Just give me a second or I'm gonna come so fast it'll be over before it begins."

A quiet pride filled her chest. "Really? Could I really make you come that fast?"

He gripped her hips harder for a second then he finally relaxed. "I've told you countless times before, you are the hottest woman I've ever been with. By far. If you wanted to make me come it would take less than a minute."

"Maybe that's exactly what I want. What I need?" The words came out in the form of a question because she really didn't know.

She wanted to make love to him for hours, but she also wanted to know how much he needed her. How much he wanted to be in bed with her, naked, silent, but saying so much.

He palmed her breast, caressing her nipple before he pinched it softly. "Fuck, baby. You can have whatever you need. Whenever you decide you want it, trust me, it's yours."

She lifted herself up, pushing on his chest to get more friction and slid back down. She squeezed the muscles in her ass to ride him. To make love to him.

Using only her hips, she made tight circles until the muscles in Michael's jaw went rigid.

Slowly, she pulled off again and paused.

"You're killing me. Fuck. Hottest wife imaginable. Best girl. Sexiest submissive. Killing me."

Tabitha bit her bottom lip and tilted her head to the side to stare down at the man she loved with all her heart.

With his hands on her hips, he helped her find the rhythm she wanted. Needed.

Up and down from her knees, she took him inside her.

His shaft throbbed as she ground her pussy onto him.

Sensation tingled in her pelvis as she worked her hips. She wanted to come on him. With him inside her. But she couldn't get enough friction just fucking him.

As if she'd asked him, Michael slipped his thumb between them. "You're so fucking wet." He jerked inside her and lifted his hips on each stroke.

"How. Did. You. Know?" Tabitha asked him as her orgasm barreled toward her. Almost there. Her heart fluttered in her chest, looking down at the man she'd given herself to so long ago.

"That you needed something else to come, Tabby?"

Her breath caught in her chest at the use of her nickname. Nothing affected her like the man beneath her. Nobody else even came close. She nodded, speeding up. The pleasure racing toward her couldn't be stopped. It could only be wallowed in.

"Because I know you." He swirled his thumb as if he were licking her clit. "I know your body, your reactions, your needs. I know my wife. My possession. And pleasuring you is the most important thing in my world."

Heat suffused her limbs and she dug her nails into his chest, making him hiss.

He lifted the hood of her clit with one hand and rubbed the sensitive nub beneath with the other.

Pleasure detonated from where he touched her and she rode his thumb and cock. "Michael," she breathed as she came.

"Fuck, baby. Come on my cock. Come on me. I'm about to explode inside you, but not until you wring every ounce of pleasure from me first. Holy shit."

He never stopped moving his thumb. Never ceased fucking up into her, even when her rhythm stumbled.

"Oh, God," she breathed as another wave of ecstasy raced

to the top of her head, making her entire body tingle.

Her lungs filled with oxygen just because it was an automatic response. The entire world zeroed in on her lover. Her husband. Her everything.

Shaking as she twitched and jerked in pleasure, she locked gazes with him.

His breath sawed in and out of his lungs and his chest had gone hard beneath her fingers.

"I love you," she whispered.

He stretched his neck, grinding his teeth together, and grabbed her hips again. He held her so tightly she'd wear his marks the next day if she was lucky.

"Love you," he told her. "So much. More than anything." He closed his eyes then stared at her again. "Thank you."

"For what?" Sensation raced up her spine and his cock throbbed inside her again.

"Loving me. Making love to me. Coming home. All of that and so much more."

Tabitha pulled his hands from her hips and laced her fingers with his. She bit her lip and swiveled her hips again. Another shiver trembled down to her toes.

A small smile lifted her lips and he shook his head.

"What's that look for? Should I be worried?"

"Maybe." Using his hands to steady herself, she tucked her feet up onto his thighs and spread her legs, sitting back on her heels each time she relaxed.

"Oh, fuck," they said together.

He slid deeper into her sex and she ground her pussy and ass against his balls on the downstroke.

"I want it," she murmured down at him, and squeezed his hands.

The vein in his neck throbbed just as his mouth fell open and his cock jerked inside her.

Short pulses of her hips sent him over the edge.

He moaned so loud it vibrated through her and he grabbed a handful of her hair and pulled her down. Crushing his mouth to hers, he came.

As she tasted his mouth he filled her pussy with his cum.

Spurt after spurt sank inside her, marking her with passion and love.

Her pussy spasmed around his pulsating shaft, making them both groan.

Tabitha's abdomen clenched so hard she ended up dislodging Michael.

Panting against him, she kissed him again.

He rolled them to the side and they both collapsed.

He fumbled for the covers, patting the bed behind him. He got them covered up just in time.

Never had she remembered being so tired. Complete exhaustion pulled at her with an unrelenting grasp. She snuggled into Michael's chest and he pulled her closer.

"Sleep, my love."

Rubbing her nose against his sternum, she breathed him in.

The disappointment from earlier tried to creep in but she pushed it back.

That feeling wasn't welcome in their bed. Never would be.

She was home. Not in the house. Not even in their bed. She was home in his arms, and she had to believe the rest would fall into place.

Not because it would magically happen, but because she was ready and willing to make it happen.

Because she wasn't walking away. Leaving wasn't what she wanted. It never would be. She'd been silent for too long. He was the man of her dreams and he was worth fighting for. *They* were worth fighting for.

Chapter Thirteen

Michael

The next morning, Michael set a steaming cup of tea down at Tabitha's place at the table just as she walked downstairs.

"Michael?" she called for him.

He closed his eyes and took a deep breath. Fuck, he liked it when she said his name.

"Dining room."

As soon as she stepped around the corner she glanced at him then at the table. Her smile fixed him like nothing else on the planet could. "You made me tea?"

He pulled out the chair for her. "Earl Grey. I wanted peppermint but we were out. Thought you might need something to warm you up this morning."

She stepped closer to him, wearing nothing but one of his T-shirts.

And underneath that shirt? Gorgeous skin with faint rope marks around her chest and arms. He'd seen them when he'd gotten out of bed a few minutes before.

They reminded him of something he wanted to talk to Wes about. The desire to learn rope so Michael could tie Tabitha had been a need for a while. And it was way past time he stopped living for tomorrow. He wasn't ready to talk to her about that just yet. They had much more pressing matters to cover.

To repair their relationship. Their trust. That took precedence over everything else.

Lifting her chin, he then kissed her.

She kissed him back, then said, "I have you. What else

could I possibly need?"

Michael stopped her before she took a seat and palmed her cheek. "You wreck me when you say things like that."

"Nothing but the truth. Ever."

He sighed against her lips. "Softest lips ever." After kissing her again, he pulled in a deep breath. Breathing her in filled him with more than just her delicious scent. She satisfied him with love and desire and more happiness than he thought he deserved.

Which brought him to the reason they had to talk.

He kissed her one more time and gestured to the chair. "Sit tight for just a second. I'm gonna grab a cup of coffee. Want anything else while I'm still up?"

She sat down and he headed back into the kitchen to the coffee pot.

"Just the tea is great."

"Sure you don't want anything to eat?" He glanced at the clock on the stove and filled his cup. "It's noon already," he called out.

"No." She glanced over at him at the doorway then looked out of the window beside the table. "My stomach's upset." Her last three soft words made more than his heart ache.

He kissed the top of her head and sat down in the chair beside her. "I'm so sorry your stomach's upset."

She shrugged then attempted a smile. "Kind of to be expected at this point."

"At this point." Michael shook his head and took a sip of his coffee before he set it down. "I can't believe I let it get to this point."

"We, my husband. We. Don't shake your head at me." She took his hand and gave it a squeeze. "We're in this relationship. Together. It's not like we have a complete power exchange where all of the responsibility falls to you. Yes, our dynamic is in place all day every day. I can't shut off what you are to me or what I am to you. I am your submissive. It's an *is*. An absolute. At home or work, cooking dinner together or sleeping, I'm always your submissive.

Even if you're asking me what movie we should rent. But that doesn't mean it would be fair of me to expect you to fix everything. It's on both of us, so we both have to make this right."

"But I fucked up, Tabitha. Me. I'm just so sorry."

"Me, too."

He scowled at her words. "You're sorry I fucked up or you're sorry for something you did?" Only the first option was going to be acceptable.

"Sorry for something."

A bit of a growl, which he normally kept in check, escaped. "What could you possibly be sorry for? You didn't do anything wrong."

"Didn't I? I knew there was something wrong. I've felt it for a while. I thought everything would be okay without facing it, which was a lie." She took a sip of her tea. "I didn't want to address it and I hoped it would just disappear. I wanted to sweep it under a rug because I didn't want to deal with it." She met his gaze. "I didn't want to acknowledge there was a problem. That we had a problem. It's naïve, I know, but I thought we were above that. Immune, maybe."

"I thought so, too," he admitted. "Thought things would just even out on their own and we could get back to where we were."

"But things changed," she continued. "And change is scary. Good or bad, altering anything like this is still scary."

"I guess you're right." He thought about it for a second. "Never really thought about it that way."

"I've been doing a lot of thinking lately."

Michael's stomach dropped. "That sounds ominous."

"I've had a lot of time to think."

He nodded, not really certain what he wanted to say, not at all certain he wanted to know what she meant by that. But this wasn't going to fix itself.

They had to do it.

And he had to start by asking the hard questions. "How close were you to leaving last night? Really leaving."

Tabitha pulled her arm back, holding onto her mug of tea, and stared out of the window again. It took her a while to answer. "Close."

"How close?"

She closed her eyes for a second and rubbed her lips together before answering. "Suitcase on the bed. Plane tickets pulled up on the laptop. It wasn't good."

He palmed her cheek, bringing her gaze back to him again. "I can't tell you how sorry I am for disappointing you." Rubbing her cheek with his thumb, he stared at her. "I've been doing a lot of that lately. Apologizing." *Disappointing you.* That 'was what he should have said, but he just didn't want to voice it.

Tabitha chewed on the inside of her cheek for a second before she continued. "Everyone has their line in the sand, I think. With relationships. And you crossed one last night."

"Not showing up last night?" he asked, which he knew was heinous.

She shook her head. "Breaking your promise."

Gut. Punch.

"But…" She started then trailed off.

"But?" Michael had never latched on to a single word so tightly in his life.

"But it's you. It's not some random person. Not a friend or an occasional lover. It's you. My husband. My Dom. The man I gave myself to and vowed…"

Michael straight up held his fucking breath.

Tears filled her eyes. One slipped free, which she quickly brushed away. "For better or worse, you know?"

Michael wanted to put his head on the table.

He wanted to get on his knees and pray, so thankful for the woman who wore his ring on her finger.

Instead, he got up, slid her chair back, scooped her up and sat back down with her in his lap.

Kissing her tears away was more than a simple gesture.

It was a vow.

A renewed vow.

Snaking her hand up behind his neck as she laid her head on his chest made everything else inside him settle.

She completed him in ways he didn't normally focus on.

That was another mistake he was going to rectify from here on out.

Before he could say anything else she swallowed and continued.

"Money isn't everything. It's not even in the top five things that are truly important to me. I'd live with you in a hammock on the beach somewhere if it meant we were together. I don't need a three-story house and a new car each year to feel special. You do that all on your own." She stared at him and smiled. "You're important. We're important. Everything else is secondary."

"You're my number-one priority. Always have been. Even with everything else. The disappointments. The missed dinners. The late…everything. Wanting to make the company a success is for us. Please believe that."

"I do believe that. I do."

He took a deep breath and rubbed her back. "But? I know there's a *but* in there."

Sitting up, she turned on his lap to stare at him. "But I need you. I need us. Money is awesome. Being successful and knowing you faced a challenge head-on and kicked its ass is even more amazing. But getting to fall asleep with you every night is what I need. Waking up with you, making love with you in the middle of the night, feeds my soul."

"Me, too. I've missed all of that. But I want the company to use the momentum we have and grow huge. I want it to be a multinational powerhouse with the ability to handle any project. And I want…" Apparently, it was his turn to look away.

Tabitha lifted his chin. "What, my husband? What do you want?"

"I want you to be proud of me." There it was. His second-biggest need, which had been messing with his biggest priority. "I need it."

Tears glittered in his wife's eyes and she smiled a second before she palmed his face and kissed him. She kissed him again and he held her close when she tried to pull away.

He breathed her air and licked his way into her mouth until she giggled.

"You have the best ways to try to distract me."

He kissed her one more time. "It was worth a try so you didn't have to address that last admission. Pretty sure they might try to take my man card away after that one."

"You needing me doesn't revoke your man card. It's one of the prerequisites for a real man. At least, it sure should be. I want your approval just as much. With little things like my latest crochet project to big things like what happened on my latest hot wife date."

He took her hand and held it. "And you have it. With all of that."

"As do you."

The look of love she gave him let him take a deep breath. And another one. "My old man told me I'd never amount to anything. I have to prove him wrong." She knew of his background but he'd intentionally never spoken very much about it.

"You prove him wrong every day. Every day you're a friend. A great husband. Being the owner of your own company is only a piece of you proving him wrong."

"Well...fuck." Talk about showing him the answer when it was right in front of his face. "You're right. As usual, my wife."

"Being right isn't what I'm looking for. Not at all."

"What are you looking for?"

"You." She shrugged. "I know it's simple, but it's the truth. I understand being preoccupied at work. But you also have to let work go so you can recharge and attack it the next day. You have to find a way to leave it at work, which I know is easier said than done. But if you can't figure out that part than something else will have to give. How I see it, the only other option is us. And..."

Yeah, he already wanted to puke as she paused, but he was the one who had fucked up. The last thing he was going to do was not let her get it all out.

She took a deep breath, as if she needed some encouragement. "Being neglected doesn't make me feel emotionally safe. Especially with our extracurricular activities. The rules—"

"Our rules," he corrected.

She smiled and punctuated it with a nod. "Our rules. Your permission to let me be me is part of our foundation. When those things disappear, so does my hold on that part of us. Sex has always been important to us. I hope it's always important to us. But we have to be on the same page or it will never last long-term. And, honestly, neither will we."

Nodding, he rubbed her back and took a minute to think. "Are we still on the same page?"

"Before last night I would have given you an emphatic yes. But everything got shaky last night. You've never broken a promise to me before. And breaking it when it comes to me being with someone else and you not being there when we were done scared me. I hate saying it. Hate owning it. But without you there to reconnect with me, to give me aftercare, especially when I'm with Wes and his edge is harder than most, it made me feel lost. I don't want to feel like that again."

"Fuck, baby. I know I messed up. Just...fuck." He pulled her close, kissing her mouth. The shiver running through her body when he held her was another gut punch. "'I'm sorry' isn't good enough for what I did last night. Leaving you in the hands of someone else to put back together is unforgiveable."

"No." She pushed back to look at him again. "I forgive you. Don't for a second think that I don't forgive you."

"Why?" The question was out of his mouth before he could stop it. He kept going because he had to know. "Why would you forgive me? What I did was even more horrible than I thought it was. And add subdrop into the equation, too."

"Several reasons, I guess. You're truly sorry, for one. And I believe you. But also, we've been together for almost six years. One bad thing doesn't negate years of the best relationship I've ever had. It's like a husband savings account you've been adding to for as long as we've been together."

"I think that's one of the nicest things I've ever heard."

She shrugged. "It's true, though. You have to admit." Her smile would have knocked him over if he hadn't been sitting. "And I am pretty amazing."

Michael chuckled and ran his fingertips along her cheek before he tugged her forward for another kiss. "Yes, you are."

"Thanks," she whispered against his mouth.

Her lips on his tasted as sweet as the vow she'd given him on their wedding day. He'd let her down, more than once. "It won't happen again," he mumbled more to himself than he meant to say it out loud.

"What won't?"

"Giving you the impression there is anything more of a top priority than you. Breaking a promise I make to you. Giving you a reason to be disappointed in me. Any of it. All of it. I give you my vow it won't happen again. I'll find a balance. I swear it."

"I believe you."

He stared at her. "Just that easy?"

She thought for a second. "No. Just that important." She wrapped her arms around his neck and whispered in his ear. "Good thing your savings account was so big, huh?"

He hugged her close. "So very good."

"And I have a thought."

"I'm all ears."

She paused and moved her arms as she sucked her lips between her teeth. "I don't think I've ever really told you how much our rules mean to me."

"I know you like them. You smile any time we joke about

them."

"They're more than just a simple list of things, though. Definitely not a joke anymore. They make me feel loved. Safe. Like you're with me all the time, even when we're apart."

"What do you mean?"

"I've kind of been thinking about making them more official. Kinda."

"That's super-hot."

Her smile was like sunshine. "Really? You don't think it's stupid?"

"That is so far from stupid they're in different countries. And I've been thinking something a bit more formal between us is way past due. You're mine. In the simplest and most complex sense of the word. Vanilla, kink, everything. Starting with our rules sounds like an amazing place to start."

She kissed him and moved off his lap with a purpose. "Hold on a second. Let me go grab something out of my purse."

"'Kay," he called after her as she ran out of the room. His cock jerked when she cleared the doorway again. "You know I want to fuck you right now, don't you?"

"You do?" She lifted the edge of her shirt, exposing her naked pussy, then straddled his lap and sat down.

"Fuck. Yes. Maybe we should have a new rule. Have all hard conversations with me inside you."

She held his shoulders and wiggled on his lap until he gritted his teeth. "That's actually what I want to talk to you about."

"Then I'm all ears." He palmed her backside and pulled her a little closer.

She glanced at his crotch and bit her lip. "All ears? That's it?"

Holding her to his chest, he stood, pushing his boxers down his legs one-handed. His cock sprang out of the fabric, slapping her pussy, and they both groaned. "Let me show you instead." 'Cause he was going to explode if he didn't get inside her. "Hottest thing ever." Bending her knees a bit, she half stood as he fisted the T-shirt out of his way.

He rubbed some spit around the head of his cock and grabbed the base, pointing his dick at the opening of her sweet pussy. As soon as she made contact, he hissed. "Fuck, you're wet. Guess I didn't need any spit."

She sat on him, taking him as deep as she could, then her entire upper body jerked. "I love it when you do that, even when I'm already wet."

"Why? It's just so I can get inside you without hurting you."

"Exactly. It's something small you do to take care of me. And it's like you're kissing me with your cock." Her smile lit his entire world. "I like that, too." She wrapped her arms around him and circled her hips.

There wasn't anything more amazing in the world than having his wife ride him, in the middle of the day, in their house, wearing his shirt.

Several silent minutes passed but they never stopped talking.

Forehead to forehead, heart to heart.

Amazing how much could be said with no words spoken.

"*Mmm*," she hummed, then something crinkled in her hand right next to his ear.

"Didn't you have something you wanted to talk about, Tabby? Or did I distract you completely?"

Her sigh bubbled up his spine, making his head tingle. She slowly opened her eyes and blinked at him. "Completely distracted."

Holding her hips, he slowed her down then stilled. "What did you bring to discuss?"

She shook her head as if she had to clear it.

His cock jerked. He was very much in lust with the idea of distracting her completely.

"I love it when you do that, too. Jerk inside me. So dirty." She loosened the hold she had around his neck and pulled her arms back between them. In her hand was a small piece of paper. She unfolded it.

The paper was worn, as if it had been read many times. "What do you have there? Looks like you've loved it, whatever it is."

"Very much so. It's our rules. Kinda."

"You wrote them down?"

"Mm-hmm. Started as a joke sort of thing. It turned into something else."

"You're shitting me?"

"Nope." She laughed. "That's not one of my kinks." She flipped the paper to the side so he could see it, too. "It's not really in any particular order. Just things we've talked about. Things we've agreed we'd do or wouldn't do. Other thoughts on things that help me."

"Our rules?"

She shrugged, lifting the paper a couple inches. "Yeah."

He took the piece of paper as if it was some sacred scroll from centuries ago. Something unearthed from hallowed ground.

"When did you do this?"

"I started it a couple years ago. Wanted to tell you about it quite a few times, but I felt kinda stupid. I'm grown and shouldn't need something like that to make me feel safe. But it turns out I did need it. Emotions have always been such a negative trigger for me."

"Your ex really did a number on you. I'm so sorry I didn't see what was happening. Sorry I didn't see that you needed more than what I was giving you."

"But you did." She glanced at the list and back up to him. "Even if you didn't know it."

Poring over the list, he vaguely saw more than a handful of things written in different colored pens. Michael had a hard time focusing on the words because he was so blown away by how she loved him. Them.

"What's the last one? I can't read it."

She glanced at the paper and bit her lip. "Charger. Not

being able to talk to you yesterday after your phone died was not awesome. Avoiding that in the future is a need."

He stared at her, somehow more in love with her than he had been the day before. The hour before. Even a minute before. "You wreck me, my wife."

"You don't think it's dumb having them written down? You really don't? Swear?"

"This is not stupid, Tabby. This is amazing." He shook his head, at a complete loss for words. "Amazing." He kicked his boxers off and stood, holding her up.

"What are you doing?"

"Wrap your legs around me."

She locked her ankles behind him and he took a few steps to the side to lay her down on an empty part of the table. The list he set next to her, the light color of the paper a stark beacon against the dark mahogany wood. A reminder of all he had to lose and everything he had to fight for.

He thrust inside her, grabbing on to her shoulders to take her harder.

"Michael?"

He stared into her eyes. "You're incredible." That was all he could say. All he had. She was incredible. How she loved them. How she was so devoted to them even with her ability to fuck other men.

She'd always kept it about them.

The other guy, even a guy as successful as Wes, was just another guy.

She'd chosen Michael even when she could have anyone.

He'd never again take her love for granted.

Lifting her legs to his shoulders, he grabbed her hips and pumped into her hard and fast. "Come for me. I need to feel you come while I'm inside you."

She grasped the edge of the table, giving him even more traction to fill her sweet sex.

"Fuck, I love how your tits bounce when I fuck you. They're the perfect size. Just like the rest of you."

Tilting her head to the side, she stared up at him.

"What's that look for, my wife?"

"Love."

One word. That was all she said. No hesitation. "How you love me floors me. I'm the luckiest man alive because I have you."

Her heels dug into his shoulders and she sucked in a sharp breath. "I love belonging to you. I'm the luckiest woman. Always. Have. Been."

He punctuated each of her last words with a hard thrust, since her pussy clamped down as she spoke.

"Oh, fuck. Fuck," she moaned. "Michael," she breathed as she locked her gaze with his.

Her orgasm triggered his own. Like lightning, pleasure raced up from his toes and down from his head and shot from the end of his cock.

She was just too exquisite not to come.

Jerking inside her, he filled her with his cum, and her body sucked every drop in. His balls pumped again and again, marking her, claiming her.

Tears rolled from her eyes and she brushed them away.

Gently shifting her legs, he leaned forward and gathered her close. He cradled her head as she wrapped her arms around him.

"Love you so much," she whispered. "I've missed this."

Michael's heart ached at her words. He wanted to deny them, make excuses even, but he just couldn't. Because he'd missed it too. Not a little bit, even. A lot. "Never again will we have to miss it, Tabitha. I won't risk us. Never again."

"And I promise to tell you in the future if I see there's something wrong. I won't let it affect us again. Not ever."

With his cock still jerking every little while, Michael lifted a bit above Tabitha so he could stare at her face and kiss her tears away. "My eyes are wide open now. I won't let it get this bad again. Promise."

Tabitha smiled. "Deal."

He stared at her a little while longer, until she took a deep breath and her arms fell down on the table. "How about I run you a bath and heat your tea and bring it to you?"

Tabitha glanced over her shoulder and laughed. "Don't think that's going to be possible."

Michael followed her gaze and chuckled, too. There was sloshed tea and coffee all over the other end of the table. "How about a bath and I'll make you some *new* tea?"

"That sounds great."

He finally pulled free of her and helped her off the wood.

"Then I'll go start the bath and you can meet me with the tea."

"You sure?" He hugged her close and kissed her mouth.

"Yep. Then maybe you can join me."

"Actually." He glanced down at the table, at her rules. "I'd like a little time with that piece of paper so I can make things a bit more concrete for us." He found her gaze again and he'd have thought he'd handed her a diamond ring the size of Jacksonville. "I take it that does it for you, my wife?"

Up on her tip toes, she kissed him. "More than I can say."

"Then you head to the bath and I'll follow in just a few minutes with new tea. Then when you're done I'll discuss a few additions to the amazeballs list you already have started. And if we agree, they'll be our rules. We'll make changes and add rules as we see fit in the future." Michael palmed her ass as she walked toward the stairs.

"I never expected today to be so wonderful. What an amazing surprise." She didn't say another word as she climbed the stairs in her birthday suit. But her giggle reached inside him a few seconds later and warmed more than just his heart.

* * * *

An hour or so later, wrapped in her purple robe, Tabitha walked out of the bathroom just as Michael was walking into their bedroom with a spiral notebook and pen in hand.

Her smile lit the room even more than the afternoon sun shining through their windows.

Fuck, how did I ever leave her feeling alone?

And for money?

He shook his head.

"What's the head shake for?"

"Just wondering how in the hell I got so lucky to have found you." Setting his pad and pen down, he then sat next to them on the bed and held his hand out for her. He pulled her forward onto his lap and she wrapped her arms around his neck.

"Fate," she answered against his lips.

"Fate. You think so?"

She nodded and ran a hand along his cheek, his jaw. "With every ounce of me."

"You shut down every thought in my head when you stare at me like that."

"Like what?"

"A woman in love."

Her smile nearly stopped his heart because almost all the worry he'd seen there for weeks was gone. It was just her again. Just them.

Deep down he'd known something was wrong. He'd never make that mistake again.

"You're my favorite thing." No idea where the admission came from, but it was out. And true.

She bit her lip and eyed his mouth. "I am?" she whispered.

Nodding at her, he pulled her a little closer. "More than anything."

Her mouth on his washed away the rest of the fear that had plagued him the night before. *Never again. Ever.*

He shifted on the bed and knocked his spiral notebook off.

Their lips popped when Tabitha pulled away. She grabbed the spiral, almost put it on the bed then stopped to do a double take. "Michael?"

"Yes, my love?" He watched her, floored by the play of emotions across her face. Humbled by it. Built back up by it into something more than he actually was.

"What is this?" she whispered.

"Our Rules." He scooped her up and adjusted them on the bed so he could lean against the headboard with her in front of him, her back to his chest. Protected.

She ran her fingers over the handwritten words on the page. "You wrote them?" Her voice caught at the end and she shook her head as if she were trying to clear it. He wondered if she thought it was a dream.

Fuck, he loved her.

"I did. All of them you already had. Adjusted a few. Added some."

"And it's all finished?"

He shook his head, staring at the page over her shoulder. "No. I don't ever want it to be finished. I want to add and alter it as things come up. What you started was amazing. I love that you told me how important it is to you. Because it's important to me. Very important. Making you feel safe is not something I will ever take lightly."

She swallowed several times and brushed at the tears on her face. "I don't know what to say."

He palmed her cheek and turned her head so he could kiss her. Soft. Gentle. Reverent even. "Read them. Out loud."

"I don't know if I can do that."

"I'll help you."

"Really?" The look on her face. Pure joy and something else he'd wondered if he'd lost. Trust.

"Absolutely. Then we can talk about them and see if we want to change anything." He kissed her again. "Fuck, I love you."

She held his face when he tried to pull back.

Her lips, her mouth, her breath. Home.

With a sigh, she ran her nose along his and held him close for another few seconds.

Breathing her in, he kissed her one more time. "I'm gonna love you forever."

"Ditto," she told him with one more kiss. She turned back around and stared at the paper again. "Oh my God, I can't believe you wrote these." She scooted back a tiny bit, putting her flush against him again.

"And I wrote them in first person. Thought you might like to type them up and we'll keep a draft accessible we both have access to."

"Can I rewrite them from my point of view, too? That way we both have a set? I can even color code mine. Make it look like a rainbow."

"I wondered if you might want to do something like that. Love that idea."

She shook her head. "Wrecked. Okay… *Number one. No panties when we're together. I want you to be accessible to me all the time.* Mmmmm. *Number two. I will always be there when a date is over. Always. And we will reconnect as quickly after as you are able. We will not separate for any reason until we are fully reconnected.*"

"Now it's a rule, so there's no leeway."

She skimmed her fingers over the words and he hugged her close. It took her a little while to continue. "*Number three. You will text me when you're going anywhere and when you arrive so I know where you are at all times. Number four. Forty-eight hours' notice for dates so we make sure we have enough time to devote to us, before and after. Changes happen, but those will be discussed verbally.* I couldn't agree more. Doing that is still all about us for me. If we don't have us, then I don't want that piece of it."

"And we'll make sure that we're on the same page, just like we always have been. It's kinky dirty fun that's awesome but we take priority. Always."

"*Number five. Each night we will check our calendar together so we both know what is happening the next day. One more way we can reconnect.* That's…" She rubbed her lips together, which he'd noticed lately was a sign she was getting emotional and trying to get it under control.

"Yes, baby?" He kissed her neck again. "Like that one, do you?"

"So very much." She swallowed a couple times and kept

reading. *"Number six. No running. If there's something we don't want to discuss then we will do it immediately. In person always preferred."* She rubbed her lips together again. "That one's going to be hard for me."

"I know. But I'll help you." He kissed her neck. "Always. Not knowing where you were terrified me. Thinking I'd lost you before I could talk to you knocked my knees out from under me. We're in this together. Completely. So, no running. And that feeds into number seven."

"We will always have a way to communicate, including our cell phones and phones at work. We will keep mobile chargers in our vehicles and at work so we are never without the ability to reach each other. Completely agree. Number eight. No breaking promises. Ever."

"Not ever again." He rubbed his lips along her neck. "You have my word, Tabby."

"Number nine. No hot wife dates at the house. Our house and our bed are ours. No one else gets to touch that part of us." She turned a tiny bit to the side. She opened her mouth to speak then looked at the list again. "Number six. I have something I don't want to talk about."

"But you have to." He grinned. "'Cause it's a rule now."

She wrinkled her nose but pressed on. "Are you mad about last week when I added my date with Wes? Or mad that I had him come to the house?"

"Nope. We discussed it. If I would have had a problem with it, I would have told you. But I saw how you wrote it on your list of rules. You had a question mark on no dates at the house so I had a feeling it was longer than just the other night that it made you feel weird. This way I just made it official so you don't have to worry about it anymore. Plus, I really like the idea of us having our own space. Work for you?"

She kissed him. Just a quick meeting of lips. "Very much so. I don't know when it changed, but it did."

"I couldn't agree more. Number ten?"

Tabitha stayed sideways and snuggled against him.

"*Condoms for all others. I'm the only one who takes you bare unless I specifically agree to it.*" She looked up at him. "But we already do that."

"Yes, we do, but I like it in writing. A lot. I'm possessive of you. Something in writing that makes you even more mine? Hell. Yes."

"*Number eleven. No lying. Ever. Our trust in each other is what makes us 'us,' and allows us to be dirty outside our relationship. Without complete honestly we are nothing.*" She nodded and closed her eyes. "I couldn't agree more. I've left a lot out lately and to me it felt like the same thing."

Michael rubbed her back. "Number five and six and eleven. Hard ones, but some of the most important. And number twelve is more of a vow than a rule."

"*I will never use your emotions against you. I repeat, I will never use your emotions against you.*" She barely got the words out. The last two came on a whisper of air.

He gave her a minute and kissed her temple. He didn't make her discuss that rule. She was raw from the day before and pushing her while she was still fragile did nothing for him.

"One more. Last one for now."

"*You will wear something of my choosing on each of your dates. Something that shows my claim on you for everyone else to see.* But I already have something." She held up her left hand. "My wedding ring says all of those things."

"Agreed. But if your hands are behind your back or over your head, it can't be seen." He reached up to circle her throat with one of his hands and stared at where he touched her. As he ran his thumb along her pulse point, he felt her heartbeat speed up.

"Like a collar?" she asked in a hushed tone.

"Very much like a collar. I'm not exactly certain what I want yet. A collar-looking collar or something else that you could wear every day. Coming to a decision about collaring you is actually one of the things I did last night when I waited up for you. I don't know why I haven't done it up to this point. But collaring you something I'm going to fix immediately. Before your next date in a few weeks."

She put the notebook on the bed and fully laid on his chest. "I can't tell you how much this means to me. All of this. The rules, the collar, us. I can't live without you."

He wrapped his arms around her and held her close. "Good. Because you're my everything. Always have been. Gonna love you forever."

"Always."

Sitting there together for a while, no words were needed.

Because together, they were whole.

Chapter Fourteen

Michael

On an evening a week later, he stood on the far side of the kitchen island when Tabitha came through the door leading in from the garage.

"Michael, are you home?" She must have already seen his car so she knew the answer, but he fucking loved the excitement lacing her voice.

"Maybe."

He had a surprise for her he'd been working on for a few hours. He'd taken most of the day off without her knowing so he could make sure it was perfect before she got home. He had a years-in-the-making kind of surprise for her.

"You're home before me. What's the occasion?" She set her purse on the counter and took the pins out of her hair.

The brown locks tumbled down past her shoulders and he just stared at her.

Black skirt, purple shirt that highlighted every single one of her curves and black strappy high heels that made his cock kick behind his slacks.

"See something you like?" she asked as she came up beside the island.

He stepped in front of her, marveling at her beauty inside and out. "No. I see something I love."

She tilted her head to the side and bit her lip. A definite sign she was right there with him in his appreciation of her sexiness.

She placed her palm on his stubbled cheek. "Mmm. Love your scruff."

Brushing a hair from her cheek, he ran his thumb across her jaw. "I have a bit of a surprise for you."

"What kind of a surprise?"

He took her hands and stepped backward, drawing her forward.

They went past the corner leading to the stairs and as soon as she glanced to the side she gasped.

"The romantic kind," he answered.

Her shaky hand covered her mouth and emotion morphed her features, stripping away the mask she showed the world. It revealed the woman he was lucky enough to get to see. The woman beneath her business suits and take-no-shit attitude. The real woman beneath. His woman.

Slowly tugging her close, he moved her in front of him and faced her toward the stairs.

A few steps in front of them, on the side, sat a candle in a little votive on the hard wood floor at the bottom of the stairs. Beside it sat a red index card with something written on it in black marker.

Several steps up on the opposite side sat another candle and another card, but this one in orange.

Then a few more steps on the right another candle with a yellow card.

All the way up the stairs they went, and he knew she couldn't see it yet, not until they reached their bedroom.

She took a deep breath. And another. "What do they say?"

He gently urged her forward to stand before the first one. "This one says, 'I love the way your hair looks…wrapped around my fist'."

"Oh, Michael." She bent and picked up the red card. Running her fingers over the words, she just gazed at him. "How amazing," she murmured. "I don't know what to say."

"You don't have to say anything. You collect my love notes and I'll read them to you."

Facing him, she stepped close and he wrapped his arms around her. Her words rumbled through him as she spoke.

"You've only read one to me and my legs are already shaky."

"No worries. I'll be behind you the whole time. I'll never let you fall."

She held on tighter.

Never had he said anything in the past week that he meant more than that handful of words. He would never again let her fall. And she believed every word of his promise.

"This is going to wreck me, isn't it?"

"If I've done my job right, it most certainly will."

"Oh, lordy."

He kissed the top of her head and breathed her in. *Talk about my very own version of crack.*

With another squeeze, she let go and turned around again. "It's almost like a proposal, but we're already married."

Talk about being more right than she knew.

"Oh, my God, I love you so much."

Leaning forward, she reached to pick up the next card and he read it over her shoulder.

"I love that you know I'm not perfect and you love me anyway."

Turning around, she faced him. "I love you so much. Nobody's perfect."

"Not true."

She looked at him and he shook his head.

"It's simply not true. You're perfect."

Tabitha opened her mouth to say something and he laid a finger across it to stop her.

"Perfect for me. So perfect. Which is all that matters." He leaned forward and kissed her mouth. Her hand on his cheek fired his blood as she licked across his lips.

His brain blinked out for a second as he got lost in her. "Next card, or I'm liable to lay you on the stairs and take you now."

"That's really not the best incentive to entice me to continue too quickly." She bobbed her eyebrows at him but turned back around and moved up the stairs to pick up another card.

He followed and stood on the step below hers with his hands on the rails, blocking her in, keeping her safe.

Twisting around a bit, she held the card so he could see it. "The way you say my name when you come. So fucking hot." The card didn't say the last part, but it was so true.

The next card read, "And *my* purr. Fuck. My purr." Yes. It did say all of that and it was underlined.

Up the stairs they went. Card after card of things he loved about her. Things he thought about all the time that he thought she needed to hear. Simple things, silly things, sexy things.

More than twenty cards were in her hands as she pushed open the door to their bedroom. A rainbow of love and lust and kink and gentleness.

A mere drop in the bucket of what she meant to him.

What he loved about her. Needed.

Only one more card remained and it was a whole sheet of paper sitting on the edge of the bed, but it covered something up.

Two somethings, actually.

Somethings he should have bought a long time ago.

Tabitha's voice shook as she uttered the single word on the last piece of paper. "Mine." She pulled away the paper and dropped all the cards at her feet.

Her gasp matched the one he'd gotten downstairs. She looked at him over her shoulder then back at the two open boxes sitting on the bed. "Michael?" Her voice shook more when she called his name.

"Yes, my love?"

"Are those what I think they are?"

"I'm not certain. What do you think they are?"

"Collars. I think they're collars."

"I totally dig smart chicks."

She swallowed and opened and closed one of her hands. She reached for the larger box and he stopped her.

"Wait."

Putting her hand down by her side, she turned to look at him.

"Before you open them, I want you naked."

"Why is that?"

There were so many answers to that question. So many things he could respond with, and they were all true. But it all boiled down to one thought and he summed it up with three little words. He closed the distance between them and started unbuttoning her blouse from the top down. "Because…I love you. You're exactly what that piece of paper says you are. Mine. And I don't want anything else touching you when I put them on you. I don't want to share any piece of this with something else. Mine."

She stared up at him.

Before long she stood naked in front of him.

"Fuck, Tabby. Hottest wife ever."

"I love it when you say that."

"Good thing. 'Cause I'm gonna say it for the rest of your life." He tugged her over to the edge of the bed and picked up the first box. "This is your play collar. The one you'll wear to bed. The one you'll wear to play. With me or any others."

The thin collar sat nestled on a bed of purple satin. Black leather, three-quarters of an inch thick, was highlighted with silver accents and a ring right in front.

She ran her fingers across the leather. "It has cat whiskers stamped all the way around."

"Yes, it does. I had it made just for you."

Which he had. Nearly a week before he'd had it commissioned to his exact specifications, and he'd picked it up that morning on the way to work. And now he needed it on her.

"And the other one?" she asked.

He picked up the other box. "Your day collar. The one you'll wear the rest of the time." It was more of a necklace. A simple silver chain with a pendant on the bottom of it. On the front, it had two interlocking hearts. On the back, an inscription. One word, but it meant everything.

"Owned," she whispered.

"For the rest of forever." He waited for her to look up at him. "Will you wear my collars? Give yourself to me in every way? For love and sex and safety and everything these collars mean to us?"

Her eyes met his, blazing with love and devotion. "Nothing would make me happier, my husband."

"And I'd like something special tonight. Just for tonight."

"Anything."

"I'd like you to wear them both. When I take you tonight, make love to you, I want to see them both and know that this is the first night of the rest of our lives as you being completely mine."

She answered, but not with words.

She purred.

He shook his head. "Luckiest man ever." He set the boxes on the bed and took her hand.

"Do you want me on my knees so you can put them on me?"

"On your knees. On the bed. You on the floor beneath me does nothing for me. It actually makes me want to punch something. You are not less than me. You've never been less than me. You'll never be less than me. Quite the opposite. Understand?"

Tabitha bit her lip and smiled. With a nod, she crawled on the bed, but with her back to him.

"Face me, beautiful."

After twisting around, she settled on her heels and looked up at him.

"I want to see your eyes when I put my collar on you for the first time. And know before I do it, it's the last time I'll ever see you without it."

"Oh, fuck," she cursed. "I'm going to wear your collar."

"For the rest of your life. Are you ready to make that kind of commitment to me?"

"More than anything." She smiled from ear to ear and

clasped her hands in her lap. "More than anything."

Her excitement, her happiness. It fed his soul.

He lifted her day collar out of the box first and clasped it behind her neck. Then her play collar, her real collar. Unfastening it, he took his time so he could remember everything. The way her skin flushed as he wrapped it around her throat. The shade of her eyes as she closed them. The feel of her breath through his shirt as he leaned close to fully collar her for the first time. She wasn't fully collared until he'd put them both on her. The one she shared with the world, hiding their dynamic in plain sight. And the one only a select few were privileged enough to see her wear.

Everything faded away but her.

The world disappeared all around them as he claimed her for the first time.

He'd been doing just that for years, and he hadn't thought the collar would be that different. Hadn't thought it could feel so significant, since his ring was on her finger every day.

But it did. It was. The connection was deeper. Stronger.

He took half a step back to stare at his wife. His property. *Fuck.*

His property.

Her gaze lifted and something had changed. Her demeanor was different. Serious. Intense.

"I, umm…have something for you, too."

Well that sure stopped him in his tracks. "You do?"

She nodded. No flirty smile, no laughter or witty banter. Whatever she had for him meant something. If her face was any indication, it meant a whole lot of something.

"And I want to talk about altering one of our rules."

"Which rule?"

Rubbing her lips together, it looked as if she fought a battle to keep her emotions in check. "Number six. No running."

It took him a few seconds and all he could get out was one word. "Okay." He wanted to say something else, but his heart was kicking so hard in his chest it made it hard to breathe.

Up on her knees, she held on to his forearms and stepped down off the bed.

She opened one of her drawers on their dresser and dug to the bottom, beneath her clothes.

He couldn't see what it was until she turned around.

She held a spiral notebook.

One he'd never seen before.

Standing before him, wearing his collars, she handed him the bound set of pages.

On the cover were purple and green flowers that made him think of their garden out back.

Nerves actually twisted his stomach as he flipped open the front cover, because he had no idea what he was going to find.

What he found was the last thing he expected. "It's empty."

She chewed on her lip and nodded several times. "But I'd like to write in it." She glanced up at him and a tear slipped free.

His heart squeezed in his chest. He flipped the cover closed again and thumbed the wetness from her cheek. "What are you going to write in there, my love?"

"I'm going to write...to you."

Overwhelmed by the need to be close to her, he handed her back the notebook, picked her up and settled them in the chair by the window with her in his lap. "To me?"

She tucked her head into the crook of his neck and he held her close. Clutching the journal to her chest, she nodded. "Like how I used to text you to tell you things. When things got hard."

He got the impression she needed to hide a bit, so instead of forcing her to look at him, he simply petted her back and waited.

"Something I realized last week is I don't want to run anymore. No. That's wrong."

Fear gripped him and it took all the self-control he had to

not push her into saying more. Taking it back.

"I still want to run, and I wonder if I'll ever get over it. Running away from things makes me feel safe. I've tried changing that, tried ignoring it, tried telling myself I didn't need it, but I just do."

He held his breath and closed his eyes, uncertain how this could possibly come back full circle to making them whole again.

She shifted on his lap.

He lifted his eyelids, afraid she would be moving off his lap, away from him. Separating herself from him again.

Her...alone.

But she didn't.

She lifted her head and her eyes were the most brilliant brown he'd ever seen. Staring at him, she paused, sucking her lips into her mouth as if she was trying to hold herself together.

Clearly overcome with emotion, she swallowed several times and breathed slowly and steadily. She sniffed and tears spilled over her lashes, but something was different. The raw emotion coming from inside her wasn't filtered.

She let it out, let it free. For the first time in their entire marriage she didn't hide it from him.

Her breathing hitched as more tears fell. "I still want to run, but I just want to change my destination."

"Where, baby? Where do you want to run to?" Hope filled him as she let him in. The words. He wanted the words.

"To you," she choked out. "I want to run to you from now on. You're my safe place. Right here. In your lap, in your arms. I have never felt as safe as I do when we're together and you surround me with your strength. Your calm."

"Fuck, baby." He held her cheeks, unable to stay separate from her pain, from her joy, any longer. He kissed her tears away. Licked them. Consumed them. "Just fuck." Kissing her lips, he poured his love into the connection. His humble thankfulness. His hope. "Nothing would make me happier than to be where you run to. Nothing would make me

happier than to be *your* everything. Because you're mine."
He kissed her again. Tasting her. Loving her.

Trailing a hand down her cheek, he then skimmed his knuckles along the pulse point on the side of her throat. The ring at the front of her collar was the perfect size as he slid a finger through it.

"Owned," she whispered. Her teeth dug into her bottom lip.

"Forever and always. You're mine to protect. Mine to keep safe. I will never forget what a gift you've given me. Five years ago, when you said 'I do' and today on your knees in front of me."

"I didn't kn-n-now," Tabitha stuttered, with a shake of her head as she fought to speak.

"Never knew what, baby?" Searching her eyes, he wondered again how he'd gotten so lucky. So blessed.

"What forever looked like. Then you walked into my life. I was so lost from that very first moment."

"As was I. But I found you. Didn't even know I was searching for you, but I always thought something was missing. Something was off. Until you, my beautiful wife. You're what I needed to be me. To be whole for the first time in my entire life. I'll never take you for granted again. On my honor as a man, and your husband, and your best friend. Being your safe place will be the greatest honor of my life. But I have a question." He slid the pad of his finger along the metal of the ring as he let it go.

Her dewy gaze flipped up to his. "Anything."

"How does the journal tie into you running to me? How does it fit into what you need? And what do you want to change about the rule?"

Glancing down at the green and purple flowers on the cover, she brushed her fingers across the surface as more emotion spilled out of her. "I know you want me to talk about things. To use my words to tell you I'm scared or lonely or that I simply need you. But that's hard for me sometimes. Sometimes the thought of actually saying certain things, even though I know I need to…it's physically painful. The instantaneous panic is so hard to control. So, I thought maybe I could write them down. Like I used to text you. Then leave it for you somewhere we agree on. This way, I'm still telling you what I need to, but I can think about what I want to say first." She sniffed again and brushed away more tears. "Not get flustered in the process and lose my train of thought."

"Does that make you telling me something seem less scary?"

She paused for a few moments and her breathing hitched in her chest.

He loved more than anything that she didn't just tell him what she thought he wanted to hear. Her contemplating the answer made him so happy he could burst.

"Yeah. It does. Not a lot, but yes. And I'm hoping in time maybe it will get easier. Then I can really talk and know that it's all gonna be okay and I don't have to freak out and panic every time. And I want to put good things in there, too. Things that make me emotional. Not just the panic type, but the good kind. The kind where I want to crawl on top of you and stay a while. I want to be better and I think this will help me get there."

"Us, baby. It's gonna help *us* get there."

"Us. I like that very much."

"And the rule, baby. What do you want to change about the rule?"

"No running. Just seeing it makes me feel scared. It's like taking away one of my lifelines. So, I want to change it to run to you. That's what I want to do, what I want to stare at when I need to see something to remind me what I need to do. It's not something I can't do anymore. It's something I very, very much want to do."

"That is hands down the most amazing thing you've said to me. Ever. Nothing would make me happier than altering that rule for us."

"Us," she sighed. "Nothing makes me happier."

Her smile? Like the first morning ray of sunshine. Warm, happy, thankful. Everything. Her happiness. That was what it was. Everything.

Picking her up, he then carried her to their bed. He laid her down and stared at her. With care, he took her journal from her and placed it on the nightstand. He treated it like the precious cargo it would carry. The vessel in which she would give herself to him again and again. He would help her finally find peace within herself. Within the amazing woman she'd become, and who he would be lucky enough to get to hold and touch and love.

Quickly he removed his clothes and climbed in bed with his Tabby.

She opened her arms to him, welcoming him home.

That was what she was to him. Home.

As he pushed inside her tight sheath, he sighed against her throat. His hands shook as he wrapped them around her. This consummation, meant more than maybe all the rest.

This time, he made love to the woman he owned. To his wife. To his best friend. It felt as if they were on hallowed ground and he would forever remember this joining together as the first of many.

Beyond a shadow of a doubt, on top of her, between her thighs, loving her, taking her...he was exactly where he belonged.

Chapter Fifteen

Michael

A few weeks later, Michael leaned forward and inhaled Tabitha's perfume as he wrapped her collar around her throat.

A friend of his across town, who he'd used several times on other projects at work, owned a machine shop. While shooting the shit one day, he'd found out the guy and his girl were kinky and he had a side business making leather goods for other kinksters in the Jacksonville area and surrounding cities.

Amazing how many kinky people lurked all over no one suspected.

He ran a finger along the leather, then latched onto the ring and brought her close. He tipped her chin up and captured her lips. Nipping them, biting them…he loved it when she moaned and her fingernails bit into the flesh of his abdomen.

The shiver that worked up her spine when he let her go fired his blood like only she could.

He released her collar and stared at the ring. *Fuck.* Another hole. A bonus hole he hadn't even known he owned on her. He was going to be fingering that hole for decades to come.

To come.

Yes, she would.

So. Fucking. Sexy.

Tabitha purred when he kissed her neck and she curled her fingers into the seams of his jeans as she held him close.

Putting her collars on her for the first time had seemed so

much like a renewal of their wedding vows. But somehow better.

Because it had been completely private. Just for them and no one else.

Tabitha had cried, her emotions spilling forth the night he'd collared her. She had blessed him with her acceptance and tears.

He'd made love to her for hours that night, and they'd both agreed it had almost seemed like the first time again. She overwhelmed him. That was what she did to him. On a daily basis. Simply overwhelmed.

"Nervous?" Michael asked as he tucked the end of her collar into the small rectangular metal loop to hold the tail secure.

"Excited," she answered a little too quickly. Then she laughed and leaned in to him. "And a little nervous."

With his hands on her shoulders, he turned her around and pulled her close, running his fingertips down her naked spine.

Standing in hotel room four-two-o, they waited for Duke to arrive.

"And why are you nervous?"

"Duke's…intense."

"Which is why you like playing with him," he reminded her. He fisted her braid and firmly pulled her hair back until she looked up at him. "Isn't that correct?"

She bit her lip and wrinkled her nose. "Yes, but he also makes me nervous."

Michael stared down at her, wondering again how in the world he'd ever let his priorities get so backassward.

He pondered her comment for a second. "You feel differently playing with Duke than playing with Wes?"

"Very different. Duke's tastes are more harsh, I guess. The last time we were together, he told me about a Valentine's date he had at that club he belongs to back in Kansas. Bloodplay in *The Library*, needles, hardcore sex."

"Damn. How did we miss talking about that?"

She lifted her lips to reveal her teeth and she laughed again. "Pretty sure your cock was in my throat two seconds after you walked into the room to see me tied to the bed. There wasn't much talking that night." Another smile. "Or the next morning."

He shrugged, completely unapologetic. "What can I say? You're the sexiest little thing ever and sometimes I can't control myself."

Her sigh rumbled through her chest into him as he hugged her again. "You say the nicest things."

They stood there for a second, just being together, and Tabitha added, "The way Duke talks to me while playing… That's another reason it's different from Wes."

"How so?"

"It's almost playful."

"Wouldn't that put you more at ease?"

"Well…no. It's deceptive. He's playful and funny and such a character with his spiky hair and inked sleeves and ears full of piercings. He doesn't take anything too seriously, then all of a sudden, he strikes with a dragontail. The act of surprising me when I least expect it makes what he does even more devastating. And he knows you."

"Of course he knows me. If he didn't know me he sure as hell wouldn't be touching you."

"No. I mean, Wes absolutely knows you, too, but it's different. I think just because he's more private about it. When Duke plays with me, he talks about you. How you love me. How you look at me. It's devastating and amazing because he knows that everything I do revolves around our relationship. Him playing into that when I'm high as a kite on pain or sex or both just wrecks me."

"Remind me to thank him when we're done today."

This time she looked up at him on her own. "Have I told you how awesome things have been? How amazing we've been since we talked?"

"In the weeks since we wrote our rules, Tabby? Since then?" He knew full well what she meant and just wanted to hear her say it.

"That's exactly when. It feels like I found you again. Us. Me, maybe. I need you and — " She shook her head. "That's it, actually. It's that simple. I just need you. You ground me and I am safe with you."

Holding her cheeks, he kissed her lips, sipping at her mouth until she sighed into him. "You very much are."

He'd planned the date between her and Duke, which coincided with Duke's visit but also had given them time to find their stride again.

"You know what else I love?" she asked.

"What?"

"That you're staying. That it's us from the beginning, in the middle, with an extra bit of dirty fun, and then us at the end. I really like that. I like you here. Especially now."

"Me, too. I like being a part of it. And there are all sorts of other things we could do in the future if you want to go back to playing alone. We can be on the phone during the date. Or Skype, even."

"That's amazingly perfect."

"I'd had the thought the other day. I think we got stuck in a little bit of a rut and we just needed a shake-up to get back on track." He kissed her again. "And just to make sure you know, I will never let us grow apart. You're it for me."

"You're it for me," she agreed. "We will never let us grow apart. I can't live without you. Seriously. That might sound pathetic but you know what?" she asked. "I don't care. I'm proudly and pathetically in love with you, my husband."

"Ditto," he added with a kiss, and thought about the room they were standing in. The same room she'd left him a sad face in. This was their way of taking it back. Not erasing it, because he never wanted to forget how he'd lost sight of them. But softening the edges maybe. Hurting her had devastated him, and he never wanted to do that ever again. "I love that you can tell me anything. Love that you want to. And the journal? It's special. Incredibly so." He glanced at the clock beside the table. "Anything else we need to cover? He'll be here in just a minute."

She rolled her lips in and rubbed them together.

"What, baby?"

Her wrinkled nose endeared her to him even more. "Will you tell me again what Wes said? I hate to think me breaking down had anything to do with him taking off. I know what he told me outside your office but something was definitely wrong."

Michael moved to the bed and took her with him, settling her on his lap. "Nothing to do with it. He seemed genuinely happy that all was well with us and that I got my head out of my ass. He said something came up that he'd been avoiding as long as he could. Something to do with his family, which he normally avoids like a new strain of Ebola. Then he said something about knots or yachts under his breath. Totally odd for him to say, but when I asked him about it he said he had to go. Cut me off mid-sentence."

"Very much not like him. I just don't want it to affect your business relationship or your friendship."

Her worried gaze twisted his insides. "You let me worry about all that. You just be the most wonderful wife ever and I'll handle the details. Nothing that happened between us made Wes freak out. He's just got something else going on. If it will make you feel better, I'll give him a few days then invite him out for a drink. How's that? Might even ask him if he has some time to come over and bring some rope. Thought I might like to learn a bit. Since my girl is a bit of a rope bunny."

Tabitha froze. "You'd do that?"

"I love seeing that look of love in your eyes. I would love to tie together. You in my rope. Hell yes. It'll take me a while to get great. If it's something you're interested in doing with me."

The tension around her eyes eased and she hugged him tight. "More than anything."

Knock, knock, knock.

Tabby looked toward the door, and Michael tugged her

face back around. "All good, Tabby?"

"Perfect." She stood and bounced up and down once.

Michael brushed her collar with his fingers. "Seems like you have something on your collar. Wonder what that could be?"

Reaching up, she touched it and tilted her head to the side. "My husband's cum. He marked it last week when he put it on me for the first time."

"Damn right he did. Must be a smart guy to know exactly what he has wrapped inside it."

"Possessive, my husband?" she asked as he unlocked the door.

"Incredibly, my hot wife." Opening the door, Michael stared at his wife a moment longer until his cock pulsed. *Luckiest. Man. Ever.*

"Can I come in and play?" Duke asked as he stepped inside.

"By all means." Michael stood aside and hugged his other best friend as he moved past. "I believe the real welcoming committee is by the bed."

"Fuck. Best friend's naked wife. Mmm… Best friend's *collared* naked wife." Duke mock glared at Michael then tossed a small bag onto the office desk. "About damn time."

Michael closed the door and locked it. "What can I say? Good things come to those who wait."

Heading straight for her, Duke didn't pause as he lifted Tabitha up and took her down on the bed.

Tabitha yelped in surprise and Michael came toward them but sat on the opposite bed. Watching her shift and twitch beneath Duke as he tongued his way south was definitely a sight to see. He knew he wouldn't be able to stay away from her for long, not when he already ached to taste her, to take her.

But he wanted to watch her, to gaze on her being touched. Tasted.

Hottest wife on the planet.

"Fuck, I've missed this beautiful sight." Duke put his

hands behind her knees, forcing her legs up and out to the side. He settled between her thighs and licked her from her asshole to her clit. Gentle, teasing.

"Oh. God." Tabitha grunted as her eyes rolled back.

"No, no, no," Duke admonished with a shake of his head between licks to her clit. "Me, Duke. You, Tabby."

Tabitha laughed then whimpered as she put her hands behind her to latch on to the edge of one of the hotel pillows. Her nipples were hard, rosy, begging to be tasted. She seemed to struggle to lift her head and stare between her thighs. "New piercing?"

Duke licked up her juicy slit again, and a tongue stud flicked into view just as Tabitha jumped. Her head fell back on the bed and she shivered as Duke licked her again.

"You're already shaking, my wife." Unable to stand it any longer, Michael edged toward her. On his knees beside her, he peered down at her splayed open for his best friend. Deliciously vulnerable with his collar around her throat. "Already that turned on, are you?"

"Duke. Fingers. Tongue. Teeth." She said more through a locked jaw but that was all he could make out.

It was all he needed.

No. That was a lie.

She was all he needed. Her pleasure. *Greatest gift in the world.*

He leaned over and he licked her closest nipple, then the other one. "And where are those fingers?" Licking her again, he added the edge of his teeth before switching back to the first rosy tip.

"Pussy, my husband. And ass," she added on a sigh. In the next breath, she clamped her teeth together again and tried to stifle a scream.

He chuckled as she thrashed beneath him. To keep her in place, he reached up and grabbed a fistful of her hair. "Duke adding a little something extra to say hello?"

"Teeth," she bit out, rubbing her feet on the bed. "Biting. Clit."

Michael loved it when all she could process were single words. Knowing her brain was completely off and all she could do was feel what he was letting someone else do to her turned him on so hard. His dick jerked and he was pretty certain pre-cum leaked. That was what she did to him. All the time.

Fuck, she turns me on.

"Let's play a game," Duke announced. He latched on to Tabitha's clit and worked her holes until her abdomen contracted. Looked as if she was almost ready to come. He pulled his fingers free and sucked both into his mouth. "Holy shit, you taste good, Tabby. I'm going to have to fuck you soon, but have some fun first."

"What kind? Game?" she asked as she jerked again.

Michael would have bet money she was no more than thirty seconds from coming. And he was quite familiar with Duke. The man definitely knew his way around a pussy. He appreciated exactly the state he left her in, which made him getting up to grab his bag that much more delicious.

"The best kind, a dirty one." Duke grinned over his shoulder and gave her a wink. "You pick a number between one and five."

Tabitha bit her lip and thought about it for a few seconds. "Four."

Duke pulled out one of his dragontails—a modified short-handled whip with a long piece of wrapped leather attached to the end resembling an arrow that terminated into a very distinct point.

It had a vicious bite with a short striking distance and Duke knew exactly how to use it.

Tabitha closed her legs slowly, as if Duke or Michael wouldn't notice.

"Oh, no, no, no, pretty Tabby." Duke stepped up and opened her legs again. "You'll definitely want to be available for this game. Michael's going to get naked and you're going to suck his cock. He's going to pinch your nipples, hard. When you can't take any more then you say, please, Michael. If you say it really sweetly he's going to let go, and I'll give you a kiss."

Duke snapped the whip in the air, which made the hair on Michael's arms stand up.

"With this. Sound fun?" Duke asked with all sorts of enthusiasm.

Michael stood up and shucked his clothes. His cock sprang out of his slacks as if it was the first time he'd ever been with a woman. He climbed back onto the bed and fisted his shaft twice, then cupped his own balls. They were heavy, full. He needed to come and soon.

"Sorta," Tabitha answered with a laugh.

"Excellent. When you two are ready. I'll leave it up to you guys." Duke unzipped his jeans, tugged them open and pulled his cock out, fucking his hand as his eyes rolled back in his head. "I'll just be over here entertaining myself."

Tabitha's sigh whispered across the head of Michael's cock, and Michael turned around to glance at her just as she peeked her tongue out to lick another drop of pre-cum off the tip of his dick.

"Oh, and sit on your hands, Tabby," Duke told her. "They'll be out of the way, and I like the idea of you having to work to get his junk. You're so tasty."

Excitement seemed to race through her as she lifted her hips and followed instructions.

Michael leaned over her, planting one hand on the far side of her head, leaving the second free to rub across her tits and abdomen and wet, wet pussy.

"Aren't you worried he's going to hit you?" Tabitha asked as she licked his balls.

"If I was worried about him hitting me, then he sure as hell wouldn't be allowed near you with any kind of weapon." He pushed two fingers in her sex and pulled them free to take a taste.

"Amen to that," Duke added.

As he looked back up to Tabitha's face Michael could have taken on the devil himself and won. The expression in her eyes would have felled a lesser man.

"No one but the best touches you, baby. Ever." He smoothed pussy juice around one nipple then the other. "Ready to play?"

She wiggled and moved her feet around. "No. Yes. Kind of. No," she added with a shout. She bounced her legs back and forth. "Get started before I change my mind."

Michael latched onto one of her nipples with a viselike grip and fed his cock into her mouth when it opened in shock, or pain, or pleasure, or some combination of all three.

"Mmm, mmm," Tabitha moaned as she sucked on Michael's cock.

He pinched harder and harder until she popped off with her first, "Please, Michael."

As Michael let go, the air sizzled as Duke yanked up his arm and brought it down, making the first stripe vertically on her stomach.

Tabitha squealed and Michael used her open mouth to feed his cock back inside again. She snaked out her wicked little tongue as he squeezed her other nipple. He wondered if she did it to distract herself from the pain as he pinched harder. He thought about asking her, but she'd always said it was so rude to talk with her mouth full. He certainly didn't want that.

He grinned and gave her a little more.

Popping off again, she yelled. "Please, Michael." Her eyes on him when she said it? Her gaze? *Damn.*

Duke brought the end of the dragontail down on her stomach again. This stripe was a little bit diagonal to the first.

Michael thought it took just a second for the pain to register and Tabitha arched off the bed, off her hands. She huffed and grunted her way through it then actively sought his cock again. That she wanted him to distract her from the pain turned him on hardcore.

His dick jerked. "You keep that up and I'm gonna come in that pretty mouth of yours."

"Good," she mumbled around his shaft then closed her eyes again.

"Fuck, you guys are hot," Duke exhaled.

Tabitha closed her lips over the head of Michael's dick and she bobbed along it as Michael lightly touched the raised marks on her stomach.

"*Ungf.*" The noises she made with him in her mouth. *Fuck.*

Trailing his fingers up along her ribs and over the swell of her breast, he waited for her muscles to tighten in anticipation.

He hated to disappoint his girl, so he rubbed over her nipple for a second then latched on hard.

She didn't last five seconds before she pulled off and gasped, "Please, Michael. Pleas—"

The end of the whip sliced through the air, snapping on her skin as Duke left another mark. This one made it look almost like a Z.

"Fuck, fuck, fuck," Tabitha cursed.

She shifted on the bed and Michael grabbed her hair with one hand and shoved his dick inside her mouth. He latched on to her other nipple again. Soft, hard, soft, hard, hard, harder. Fucking her throat while she tried not to move away from either of them flipped some kind of switch inside him.

He yanked her off when she gagged and gasped for breath, not once relaxing the grip he had on her tit.

"Please, Michael," she begged before he released her, got both fists in her hair and worked his dick back inside her mouth.

The whistle and snap of the whip sounded far off to Michael as he face-fucked his wife. Her scream around his shaft nearly triggered his orgasm.

"Open your eyes," Duke ordered as he shoved his jeans lower on his hips. He ripped off his black T-shirt, tossed it onto the floor and crawled between her thighs.

Tabitha's eyelids fluttered open and she tried to look sideways at Duke as he ripped open a condom package and rolled it on.

"No. At your husband."

Her gaze immediately flipped up to his, ensnaring Michael with her stare. Her eyes were dilated with pain and pleasure.

"He's the reason I get to do this." Duke pushed in deep. "So tight. Fuck." Duke fucked into her and it jostled her mouth on Michael's dick.

"Jesus," Michael mumbled.

"You make Michael come and I'm gonna come, but you first, Tabby."

Michael relaxed one of his fists so he could use his fingers to tease her very red nipples. He glanced to the side as Duke used one hand to lift the hood off Tabitha's clit. Then he licked his thumb and rubbed it back and forth on her sensitive nub.

Groans from deep inside her broke free each time she took a breath, and a few seconds later she started to come. Her body jerked, her breathing got choppy and she twitched one of her hands. The one closest to Michael.

He thought maybe she was going to push one of them away.

No.

Instead, she reached beneath him and cupped his balls. A whisper of sensation across the taut skin of his sac and he couldn't fight it any more.

Lightning zapped down his spine and up from the pits of some ethereal place called nirvana, and pleasure exploded from the tip of his cock.

Tabitha gagged once when it hit her in the back of the throat.

He tried to pull out, because the sensations were almost too much, but she half twisted on the bed and used both hands to hold his hips to her.

She greedily drank him down as Duke grunted between her thighs. "Fuck," Duke cursed as his rhythm seemed to stutter.

Michael knew exactly how Duke felt as he closed his eyes

and let his wife drain him dry.

After Tabitha sucked the last of the cum from his balls, she collapsed back onto the bed and he fell next to her.

He pulled her against his side with her head on his chest as Duke stumbled off the bed. "That is some kind of magic pussy you got going on there, Tabby."

"And a magic mouth. Don't forget the magic mouth," Michael added with a shake of his head. "Magic everything." He tipped her chin up and kissed her mouth before they collapsed again.

"You guys are the magic. Oh, my God. I think I finally understand that phrase *la petite mort* now. I'm pretty sure I died a little when I came."

Sounded like Duke disposed of the condom in the bathroom and washed up before collapsing on the bed on the other side of Tabby. He rubbed himself on her hip for a second then relaxed. "Holy shit," he huffed out. "You guys should so totally move back to Kansas."

They laughed and Michael kissed Tabitha on the forehead and held her close.

They all three lay there on the bed for a few minutes, trying to catch their breath.

Tabitha was actually the first one to speak. "You never hit my pussy, Duke."

"Of course not. But you thought I was going to. And I got to stare as your pretty pussy got wetter and wetter, and you were ready for me as soon as you took the last hit. Great game, huh?"

"Epic game, brother."

Duke stretched and settled with his hands behind his head. "I aim to please." He smiled. "Have either of you noticed what it is?"

"What, what is?" Tabitha asked as she stretched.

"The mark on your stomach. It's a present."

"A present?" she asked as she and Michael both shifted so they could see the raised marks. "It's an M," Tabitha whispered, completely in awe.

"Exactly. My present to you guys for the collaring and working everything out. 'Cause you're awesome people and you deserve happiness. Shit tons of it."

"Leave it to you to find the perfect present." Michael ran his fingers over the marks, making Tabby shudder.

As Duke moved off the bed and went into the bathroom, Michael positioned himself between Tabitha's thighs so he could see it right side up. His cock jerked back to life, filling with an all-consuming need to possess her. He needed to fuck her. Needed it.

Running his cockhead around her wet pussy, he then pushed in semi-hard. He couldn't wait. Not anymore. He needed her.

Almost instantly his cock filled, and he thrust inside over and over, feeling every inch of naked flesh within the walls of her slick sex. Knowing he was the only one who might fuck her without a condom again lit a possessive fire inside him. *Mine*, he wanted to growl, but he only let a little snarl out instead.

What did Tabitha do?

She purred.

Duke came out of the bathroom and headed to the side of the bed Tabitha was on. He bent over and licked her sore nipples, making her squeak. "I'm getting out of here before I catch your matrimonial bliss. Michael, lock the door behind me." Duke kissed Tabitha on the mouth and lingered for a second. "Ugh. No. Bliss encroaching." He grabbed Michael by the arm and literally pulled him away. "I'll call you guys tomorrow and we can eat dinner before I fly back. Bella Luna?" Duke asked with a grin over Michael's shoulder at Tabitha. "I feel the need to add a little of my magic to your favorite restaurant. You dirty girl."

Michael chuckled and tried not to growl at his best friend.

"Sounds like a date," Tabitha answered.

"Sweet." Duke grabbed Michael by the back of the neck and pulled him close to whisper in his ear, "Luckiest man ever. Don't you forget it again."

"I won't." Michael pushed him off and opened the door, trying his best to keep his junk hidden as Duke grabbed his bag.

"Bye, beautiful," he called to Tabitha with a wink.

She stretched, her legs flopping open, revealing her well-used pussy and a peak at an ass that was all his to do with as he pleased. "Bye, Duke."

Duke saluted Michael and headed out with a wink.

Michael vaguely noticed how dark it had gotten as he shut and locked the door. He was back on the bed in less than five seconds.

"Inside you. I have to be inside you."

"Need. You," Tabitha admitted as if she couldn't catch her breath.

Everything else around them disappeared from his mind. All of it. The room, the furniture, Duke, everything.

His desperation to get inside her showed as a small shot of clear fluid pulsed from his cock.

Tabitha jerked and moaned as he lined the head of his cock up to her ass.

"Fuck. Wait. Don't want to hurt you." He went to the bathroom and grabbed the bottle of lube. He squeezed a liberal amount on his hand and fisted his cock to spread it around. Back on the bed, he tossed the lube onto the other bed in case he needed it again.

Lined up to her ass, he shoved her legs back, exposing her holes to him. *His* holes. With a growl, he pushed in until the head popped past her tight ring of muscles.

Her nails dug into his thighs. He thought it was as she processed his pain. And pleasure. She thrashed her head back and forth, trying to fight the delicious agony, maybe, or the possession. Whatever it was, she took it, took him, as he slid in with one smooth thrust.

"Can't wait." He put her ankles to his shoulders. "Hold on to me," he told her as he grasped her thighs.

She latched on to his wrists and held on. "Always," was her answer.

He rubbed a slick thumb across her clit. Her ass latched on to him as he pulled back out.

"Not. Gonna. Take. Long," she bit out as he fucked her.

In and out, he fucked her. Loved her. Took her. "Me, either, baby." He looked down at the M on her stomach and pleasure tingled in his balls all the way to the top of his head. "I love the way he marked you."

Seeing the mark, she smiled and her mouth fell open. "Oh, my gawd. It's almost like a brand right now. With the raised skin."

"So hot. Don't get any thoughts, though. A brand to your skin would do nothing but make me homicidal."

"No. Not a brand. But ink maybe?" She rubbed her lips together and glanced up at him.

"Ink? Really?"

She nodded a couple of times. "I've been thinking about it for a while now. Maybe something cute and flowery and feminine, because it makes me feel sexy. Maybe something permanently declaring me as yours. Or some kind of cute couples tattoos we could both get if you were interested."

"Fuck. It just keeps happening." He thrust faster, fucking into her because he had to give her his cum. He had to fill her.

"What?" she gasped as her nails dug into his wrists.

"Loving you more." Thrusting into Tabitha's ass, he relished every moment inside her. His balls sucked up tight to his body, more than ready to fill her with his cum. "I don't think it can happen but it just does. Often."

"So, you like the idea of ink? On me?"

"On us. Fuck. Love it so much. We'll find something perfect for us and we'll get it together. Holy shit, do I love our firsts."

"Me. Too," she added as her ankles dug into his shoulders.

He leaned forward, keeping her exactly where he wanted her. He slid his thumb on her clit, stimulating the hypersensitive bundle of nerves until her mouth fell open and her gaze locked with his.

"Mine," he growled as his first pump of cum jetted deep.

"Yours," she exhaled a second before she cried out, "I'm coming."

Michael's nerve endings lit up on every inch of his body as if a supernova had ignited along his spine. Pleasure raced to his cock as he came in her spasming ass again and again. Maneuvering her legs beside him, he laid on top of her, gathering her close to be as connected as two people could be.

He took her mouth and touched along her collar until he found the ring. Grabbing it with one finger, he trapped her next to him as she came on him and he inside her.

She clung to his back and hips and hugged him to her.

No other words were spoken as they moved together.

None were needed.

Several long minutes later, he ran his nose along the column of her throat and kissed beside the collar at her pulse point.

Life, that was what she had become. A reason for living, for working and striving to be better. Because she deserved that for everything she gave him. Everything they were.

Slowly he pulled out of her ass and she jerked.

"So sensitive," she moaned then giggled.

Giggling after she came? He shook his head. She was his perfect mate. Just was. No question about it. "Be right back."

"Uhh…" was all he got back.

He stumbled into the bathroom. He washed off his cock and wetted a hand towel with warm water. He cleaned her, too, and she seemed to watch him through sleepy eyes.

After he turned the lights off, he collapsed back into bed and maneuvered the comforter above them in the dark.

He gathered her close, face to face beneath the covers with nothing but love between them. Devotion. They moved closer, winding their legs together, and moonlight shining through the window bounced off one of the metal loops on her collar.

He ran a finger through the loop and pulled her close for

a kiss. "I didn't know," he told her with a shake of his head.

"Didn't know what, my husband?" She relaxed against the pillow and ran her fingers over his skin.

"How badly I needed this around your throat."

"So did I."

"And tomorrow I'm going to change number thirteen."

Her smile was brighter than the moon. "You are?"

He nodded. "Can't believe I didn't see it before."

"What?"

"I need you in it. Each night when you sleep. I'll put it on you at night and I'll remove it in the morning. I had no idea the meaning of possessive before I put this on you. Now I do. You're mine and I'll do everything in my power to take care of you for the rest of your life."

She sighed and wrapped her leg tighter around his. "There is nothing that can stop me from reveling in exactly what I am. What I've always been meant to be."

Michael palmed her cheek, staring into the eyes of the only woman he ever wanted to own. "Which is?"

She sighed and shifted closer until her lips touched his. On a breath of air she tied herself to him for the rest of forever. "Yours."

Epilogue

Michael

Michael stepped into his favorite neighborhood kind of bar, scanning the inhabitants for Wes. Weeks had passed with no contact. Almost two months with nothing but clipped text messages and leaving him voicemails that had gone unanswered.

He could admit to worrying about losing his friendship over his fuck-up months ago. Not that it was easy for him to say, but he was glad it had happened. And he was even more glad it had been Wes everything had gone down with.

He could count on trusting Wes to tell him when he was being an asshole.

He'd needed a big ole kick in the ass to get his priorities back on track. Money wasn't his top priority. It couldn't be. Not ever.

Not when he had the sexiest wife on the planet who was completely devoted to him, in love with him. And all she asked in return was the same — devotion, acceptance, trust, freedom, love.

Sharing her had always turned him on, but he'd wondered if it wasn't something she'd done for him instead of with him. There was a very big distinction between the two and he hadn't realized, until everything had crashed and burned, how much he'd needed it to be them in it together. And he did. Knowing she wanted it as badly as he did, craved it as badly as he did, turned him on so hard she was probably going to be sore for a couple of days.

He'd picked her up on a whim and taken her to lunch

earlier that day. Fucked her in that pinstriped skirt she loved to wear that cupped her ass like one of her lovers. Enchanting as fuck. Then he'd told her about a date he'd set up for the following weekend. Something kinky. Something delicious. She'd come on his cock so hard he'd had to cover her mouth to keep her quiet.

They had been in the restaurant bathroom when it had happened.

Michael made a mental note to carry a gag with him in the car. He never knew when the mood would strike him.

Them.

No one said having a hot wife would be easy. Michael smiled. Yet, it was worth every delicious bump in the road. He and Tabitha had never been closer, more secure in their love for each other, their commitment to their marriage and the freedom their sex life afforded them.

Glancing around, Michael was about to give up when he spotted Wes perched on a barstool, nursing a beer.

It didn't take him half a minute to weave around the rest of the tables between him and the bar. "Dude, what the fuck?" He clapped Wes on the back as he sat down. "Haven't seen you for weeks and then out of the blue you call and say you need to meet. And here of all places." He glanced around again. "It's not exactly the kind of place I expected to find you in." Wes never looked over at him. Not once. He continued to stare at his reflection in the mirror behind the bar. And his hair was a bit disheveled. "Wait. You're not even wearing a tie. What's going on? Did hell freeze over while you were away and I missed the memo?"

Wes took a drink of his beer and polished it off. That was on top of the two other beer bottles sitting in front of him which he must have already downed.

Thankfully the bartender walked up at that moment. "Whatcha havin'?"

Michael eyed Wes again, who still hadn't spoken, and faced the guy behind the bar. "Same as him. Go ahead and bring him another, too. Think he needs it."

The guy nodded, none too ruffled, snagged Wes' empties then walked to the cooler.

"Sorry I didn't call." Wes pushed the words out and he sounded tired.

"We were getting worried about you. Wondered if we were going to have to call the cops for a wellness check to make sure you didn't croak in that high rise you call a condo."

Wes lifted his lips in a feeble attempt at a smile but his mouth quickly resumed its grim line.

The bartender returned with two beers and popped the tops on them before he walked away to wait on somebody else.

Wes didn't hesitate. He pounded his beer as if it was the elixir of life and he needed it to survive.

"I didn't think you really drank. And especially not beer." Michael took a drink and set it back on the worn wood in front of him. "Take up competitive drinking while you were..." Michael blinked, then blinked again.

The neon signs above the bar glinted off something on Wes' hand. Something new. Something —

"Holy shit, Wes. Is that a wedding ring?" Yes, he barked it out a little too loudly. No, he couldn't have reined it in any more than he did. "A real wedding ring? What the fuck happened in the last few weeks?"

"I got married."

Michael's brain was not helping him out. Not at all. It just kept coughing up *what the fuck*, which wasn't going to get him anywhere. He took a deep breath, another swallow of beer and tried again. "To who?"

"A mousy girl named Macey. Who was a virgin on our wedding night." He picked up his latest glass bottle and saluted.

"Why?"

"Why was she a virgin?" Wes looked at him sideways.

"No. Why did you get married?"

"To claim my inheritance, I had to get married. And to

claim my inheritance, I had to marry her."

"That's…" Michael took a second to weigh his words. "Fucked up."

"Tell me about it."

"Wait. You haven't responded to any of my texts about fucking Tabitha. Are you off the playing field now? Jesus. Have you talked to…your wife about any of this? Had a discussion about hot wives and you being a third or anything?"

"Not. A. Word," Wes enunciated each syllable with a shake of his head.

"This Macey woman, does she know you're kinky? Does she have any idea about your allergic reaction to monogamy? Or even the concept of being a hot wife? Holy fuck."

Shooting him a glance with his upper lip curled, Wes lifted the glass bottle to his lips again and took a big pull.

"Oh. Shit." Wes wouldn't make it. He'd explode. Just watching him with Tabitha, Michael had known the guy had some demons. He'd never unintentionally hurt anyone, much less a woman in his care. But his dominant side wasn't something he could just turn off. Probably ever. "What are you going to do?"

Wes downed the rest of the bitter liquid in his bottle and slammed it on the wood with a bit more force than necessary. Torment shone through his eyes as he locked his gaze on Michael. "Nothing. I'm so fucked."

More books from Totally Bound Publishing

Book one in the Brewing Passion series

One hot entrepreneur plus a driven saleswoman and sultry brewer – simmered in the craft beer world for a unique, sexy reading experience!

Part of the Totally 5 Star collection

Who knew lies and billionaires were an explosive combination?

Shy and serious by day – insatiable by night.

Book two in the Surface Tension serial

When fiery passion can turn on a dime, how far would you dare to gamble your heart?

About the Author

Jennifer Kacey

Jennifer Kacey is a writer, mother, and business owner living with her miniman in Texas. She sings in the shower, plays piano in her dreams, and has to have a different color of nail polish every week. She's an Amazon top seller and award winning author.

Everything she writes is a little bit dark and a whole lotta naughty! She pushes the boundaries in each of her books and hopes her characters stay with you long after the last page of each story is read.

The best advice she's ever been given? Find the real you and never settle for anything less.

Jennifer Kacey loves to hear from readers. You can find contact information, website details and an author profile page at https://www.totallybound.com/

Home of Erotic Romance